SNOWED IN WITH THE GRIZZLY

OBSESSED MOUNTAIN MATES

ARIANA HAWKES

Imprint: Independently published

ISBN: 9798860534001

Cover art: Thunderface Design

www.arianahawkes.com

Rowan

*W*hen I heave open my front door, a blast of snowy air tears right through my clothes.

"You're three hours too early, you know that?" I tell the snowflakes that land on my hair and face like icy little pinpricks as I fumble with my coat buttons. Guess they didn't pay attention to the weather forecast, which said no snow before two p.m.

My little car is already covered in a white frosting. I heave my weekend bag into the trunk, then I climb into the driver's seat and tap the destination into my GPS.

ETA three hours and seven minutes. Long drive in this weather. But as long as the snow doesn't get any worse, I should still make it to Wilder's Edge well before nightfall. And if it does… well, I'll just have to deal with it. I need this vacation more than I can say. It's my last weekend of freedom, before my life gets turned completely upside down—

But I'm not going to think about that now.

I'm going to stay focused on the positives and make sure I enjoy this trip to the max.

The car's ancient engine judders as I start it up. I pull out of the driveway, turn on my left blinker, and… stamp on the brake as a sleek silver car cuts off my exit.

"Be careful, goddamnit!" a furious face bawls through the open window.

"Sorry," I mutter automatically, my throat clenching.

The driver's side door swings open and my father's tall, suited figure steps out of the car and stomps over to me. His red face fills the driver's side window. "Stupid fuc—"

I try to tune his words out. I'm either a smartass or spectacularly dumb, depending on which mood he's in.

"I need you to pick up Charlie from tennis practice. She finished fifteen minutes ago." He spits out the second sentence like that's my fault.

I blink. He knows I'm driving to Wilder's Edge today. It was the one concession he gave me. "I'm sorry, Daddy, I can't. The snow's come in early and I need to leave right now if I don't want to get caught in a blizzard—"

"I need to get to a meeting." He cuts me off.

"Can't you ask—?"

He grinds his teeth, then he treats me to his *look*. The one that makes me feel as low as a worm. The one that's usually accompanied by the observation, *you're weak, like your mother.* "What kind of sister are you, huh?"

My shoulders slump. He knows exactly how to get to me. I'll do anything for my kid sister, no question.

"Fine," I tell him, through a clenched jaw. "I'll pick her up right now."

He grunts. Then, without a word he turns and heads back to his car.

I take three deep, calming breaths, then I floor the accelerator.

* * *

CHARLIE'S glossy auburn head is nowhere to be seen. But there's Brianna, the mom of one of her teammates, standing in the entrance of the sports hall. They must be late finishing.

It's okay, I tell myself. As long as I leave in the next half hour, I'll still be able to make it. I won't wind up spending the weekend in a truck-stop motel, waiting out the blizzard.

But the sky is low and ominous and I feel like the storm could come at any moment. My eyes prickle. What if I don't make it there at all? I'll never see my Grandma Jo's old place again.

Because in four days' time, I'm going to become the property of a man I barely know.

Vincent DiMarco is forty-five years old, wealthy, and my father's biggest creditor—

Because it turns out that Daddy is not quite the successful businessman that everyone believed. He's been racking up massive debts over the years, borrowing money to pay back loans, until it's all finally caught up with him.

Now DiMarco wants to collect. He's willing to forgive all my father's debts, in exchange for *me*.

I always knew that my life would be one of duty—working for my father and his business empire. But I never saw *this* kind of duty coming. Giving myself—mind, body and soul—to a much older man, in exchange for my father's financial freedom. I can't refuse though. Because, in exchange for doing this, Daddy has promised to give Charlie her freedom, and let her live a life of her own choosing. And that's all I want. Not just because I love my little sister to bits, but because I also promised our mom that I'd always protect her.

It was a promise I made on her deathbed, five years ago, and nothing could make me go back on it—

A tear falls down my cheek. I swipe at it angrily and bite down on my tongue.

I can't cry. I need to be strong.

For Charlie's sake.

Wilder's Edge.

Keep thinking about Wilder's Edge.

Grandma Jo's adorably rustic log cabin, up in the mountains, right beside a lake. Far enough from the nearest town to have privacy, but close enough to drive for essentials. I'm going to read and sleep and hike in nature, and not think about anything else at all, for three blissful days.

Kids are starting to drift out of the sports hall, and if

I'm not mistaken, the snow is falling faster now. I turn up the speed on my wipers, and look for Charlie, knowing she's not expecting to see my car.

There she is at last—long hair tied back in a ponytail and nose red from the cold, chatting to a couple of other kids. She's a junior tennis prodigy with a fearsome backhand, but right now, she looks small and vulnerable. My heart aches for her, and I double down on my promise that nothing will ever hurt that sunny nature of hers.

I sound my horn. Charlie's head snaps in my direction, then she comes running over, a radiant smile lighting up her face.

"Rowan!" she bounds into the car with her usual puppyish energy, bringing a waft of freezing air with her. "I thought you'd left already!"

"Surprise!" I inject enthusiasm into my voice. It's not so hard—seeing my sister always lifts my spirits.

But Charlie's huge blue eyes peer into my own, and her smile drops. "Something's happened, hasn't it?"

"No. Nothing's happened."

"Dad was supposed to be here—" she trails off. Dad letting us down has been the backing track to our lives for as long as we can remember.

"Something came up. He had to go to a meeting."

"But Rowan, this is your weekend. Your break before—"

"It's fine, it's fine," I reassure her, but her eyes are brimming with tears.

"It's not fair!" she bursts out.

"Relax. I've got plenty of time. It's only three hours to Wilder's Edge." I put the car in drive and pull off.

Five minutes later, we're turning into the Ice Princess drive-thru for Charlie's favorite—a peppermint white hot chocolate. I'm desperate to cheer her up before she has to go home to our dad for the weekend.

"Rowan!" Charlie shrieks, when she figures out what's going on. "This is gonna make you even later."

"Only a few minutes, and it's worth it to spend a little more time with my baby sis." I get her in a headlock and ruffle her hair, like I used to when we were kids.

"Stop!" She fights me off, giggling. "I feel bad though."

"No arguments," I say, but when I see the line, I suppress a sigh. I'll be delayed by another ten minutes at least. And I must be the biggest klutz in the universe, because somehow I manage to pull up way too close to the window. And when I reverse, the car behind me is somehow edging forward, and… *bump!*

Darn.

"What the fuck?" bellows a voice from behind me.

With a groan, I leap out and race around to the back of the car.

It's fine. I hit the other car's bumper. Not a single mark on it.

"Goddamn woman driver!" the other driver screams, face purple.

"I'm sorry!" My voice comes out as a squeak. "There's no damage to your car though."

"What the hell were you doing?" His voice is getting

louder.

"I said I'm sorry!"

"She was reversing, you jerk-off!" Charlie's voice cuts through, loud and clear as she darts over to join me. "Which you would've seen if you were paying attention!"

He growls and snarls a bunch, but Charlie is already pulling me back to the car.

"Don't worry about him," she says, squeezing my hand until I quit shaking.

Thanks, sis," I say, beyond touched. "But, Charlie Anderson, where on earth did you learn language like that?"

She flips her ponytail. "At school," she replies nonchalantly. I blow out a breath of relief, then laugh. She's sassier than me. Better able to handle our dad.

I park up in the lot and we take a minute to sip the hot chocolates, staring out at the morning traffic as it snakes through the snow.

"You don't have to go through with this," she says.

"Huh?" I lick foam off my upper lip.

"The *arrangement*. We can just leave—"

"No." I cut her off. "It's decided."

Out of the corner of my eye, I see her body slump. When her eyes meet mine again, they're glistening with tears. "Have fun this weekend, Rowan. Make the most of every moment. You deserve it, more than anyone."

I blink back tears of my own. "C'mere." I pull her into my arms and hug her hard. "Don't worry about me. I'm tough, and I'll be back soon."

She shudders. "But you'll be—" She doesn't finish the

sentence.

Imprisoned.

Living in another town.

The property of Vincent DiMarco.

I have no idea how often we'll be able to see each other. But she'll be free, and that's what counts.

"I love you, Charl," I whisper.

"I love you too, big sis. And say hello to grandma."

I close my eyes for a beat. Charlie didn't get to spend much time with Grandma Jo. I'll always be sad that she didn't get to know her better. But I'm so touched by the way she talks about her and always wants to hear stories about the times we spent together.

* * *

I TURNED off the engine while I let Charlie out of the car and hugged her goodbye, and now it's struggling to start.

"Come on, old girl," I mutter, counting to ten before I try again. I'm already an hour later than I planned to be— *Vrooom!...* it roars to life at last.

Thank goodness. Relief pours through me. I step on the gas and drive off before anything else can go wrong.

I'll be fine. I should still arrive in Wilder's Edge before the storm hits. I put my all-time favorite playlist on the stereo, turn up the heat, and hit the road.

I'm dreaming about getting to the cabin, settling in, and cooking some dinner. I can't wait to see the old place again. Last time I was there, I was sixteen, and that week with Grandma Jo was the happiest week of my life. My mom died when I was eight, and my dad wasn't on good terms with his mother-in-law, so I didn't see much of her when I was growing up. But this week arrived in my life like a gift. My dad was away on business and his hired help quit on him, so he sent me to Wilder's Edge instead.

Grandma Jo was the kindest, funniest person, full of stories about all the fun she and my mom used to have together. She opened my eyes to a whole new world of love and laughter. She promised to persuade my father to let me visit her every year. All that long winter, the thought of staying with her kept me going through my dad's rages and mood-swings. I started to plot a way for Charlie and me to move there permanently.

And then Grandma Jo died in a freak accident. Her car went off the road into a ravine. It was good weather. There was no collision, no witnesses. It was so weird. A wave of grief hits me for the hundredth time. I still miss her so much every day. She and my mom both.

THREE AND A HALF HOURS LATER, I pass a sign saying, *Welcome to Wilder's Edge!* My heart gives a little jump. My shoulders are stiff and my eyes are burning. The snow has continued the entire way, and I've had to drive real carefully on these narrow mountain roads. I made it before nightfall, officially. But the sun has already slipped behind the mountain tops, and the road is dark as I take the final turn that leads me to my destination. And I pull up short—

Because the building in front of me is nothing like the cozy log cabin I remember.

I peer through the deepening gloom in confusion.

It's a dilapidated shack. Broken down. Barely hanging together.

This can't be it. Did I make a mistake with the GPS? I grab my phone and examine it. Nope. Correct location.

I reach into the glove box and pull out an old photo I took when I was staying at the cabin last time. There's Grandma Jo, sitting on the deck with a cup of coffee, laughing. Yup, same deck, same window frames, same door. This is it, alright.

My heart sinks to my boots.

Her lovely cozy place, ruined.

I was expecting it to be a bit run down, but not like this. The poor old thing looks like a hurricane's run through it.

Crap. Crap. Crap.

I brought a bunch of supplies and bedding with me, but this I was not prepared for, at all.

I get out of the car and gingerly climb the three steps to the decking. The wood's all rotten, but it holds my weight at least. I take my key and turn it in the lock. It's rusty, but it grates open. Holding my breath, I swing the door wide.

Wow, it's cold in here, and it smells of damp. Clearly, no one's been here for a long, long time. I can feel the wind blowing in through the cracked window panes.

I traipse through the cabin, my feet getting heavier and heavier.

Those stupid fantasies I had about curling up in bed, reading in the firelight. So naïve.

I'm more likely to wind up with hypothermia.

I can't stay here. I'll have to get back in my car and get back down the mountain as fast as I can. Forget the whole thing.

What a dumb idea this was!

What difference is four days going to make anyways, when I'm going to spend the next forty-plus years in prison?

I plunk down on the bed and take in the cabin gloomily, as I picture my father's reaction.

"Didn't make it, huh? Got a bit much for you? You never were good at taking care of yourself, Rowan."

At least the bed still seems solid enough. It has a wooden, king-size frame, and the mattress is wrapped in plastic. Grandma Jo and I used to share it when I stayed. She told the best bedtime stories, and we'd sometimes have breakfast in bed in the mornings.

A little spark of warmth blooms in my heart.

There's the fireplace, on the far side of the room. I don't know a whole lot about fires, but I'm guessing it's still operational. Maybe if I built it up real big, it'll be enough to chase out the drafts?

I reach for a light switch. The power is supposed to be connected… it is. A lightbulb flares above my head. Okay, I have electricity. This is real good.

Come on, Rowan, I tell myself. This is the last chance I'll have to spend some time on my own. Am I gonna let a little cold defeat me?

I passed Twin Falls on the way here. It's a small

town, but there was a little main street with a bunch of shops. Maybe I can swing by, pick up some stuff to make the place more comfortable.

I leap to my feet, charge outside, and head for my car again. And…

The dang thing won't start. The engine coughs and coughs, but it won't turn over. I try again, and again… but, *nada*.

So much for that idea. I drop my head to the steering wheel.

Now it's really going to be a brutal night.

When I lift my head again, I spot something in the distance—another cabin, maybe a couple of hundred yards away. Weird. I don't remember it being here before. Anyway—

Time for plan C.

I get out of the car and start walking. The snow is getting heavier now. The wind stings my face and I can feel the blizzard approaching. But lights are glowing from the windows of the cabin. It looks cozy and welcoming. Fingers crossed that's the case. There's a big black truck parked out the front. Looks like the owner's home.

I walk up to the solid wooden front door and knock.

No answer.

I wait for a minute and knock again, but no one comes.

There goes that idea.

Heaviness weighs me down.

But as I turn to leave, the wind drops and I hear a thud. I go still.

There's another, and another, coming from behind the house.

What *is* that?

It sounds violent. I feel uneasy, but I follow it anyway.

I creep around the corner, and… freeze.

Because there's a bare-chested man, swinging an axe. He has his back to me, but as I approach, he swivels around, axe in hand.

A gasp dies on my lips.

He's huge, tall, musclebound. In a daze, I take in tousled dark hair, a scruffy beard and a pair of blazing eyes—which are fixed on me. He's the most handsome man I've seen in my life. And he's outside, shirtless, in the dead of winter.

His eyes get fiercer as he takes me in, almost glowing in the dim light.

I should run. Some primitive part of my brain is telling me so. We're in the middle of nowhere. He's massive. There's a deadly weapon in his hand. And a predatory look in his eyes.

Any sane person would be running in the opposite direction.

But I don't.

I just stand there and *stare.*

"Finally," he says. His voice is low and hoarse, as if he hasn't spoken in a long time. But the word pours out of him like relief. His eyes continue to burn into mine, and he takes a step toward me.

I hold still, heart fluttering like a bird's.

2

Jaxton

My animal twitches beneath my skin as I take in this vision. I can hardly believe my eyes. I've waited for this moment for four long years, part of me doubting I'd ever see her again.

The last time I laid eyes on this angel, she was a teenager, visiting her grandma in Wilder's Edge. I was captivated. She was beautiful. So blonde and pretty and delicate. And my bear knew right away—she's my mate.

I longed to approach her. But I was a beast. I lived like a savage in the forest and I could barely speak in full sentences. I'd spent most of my life in my animal form, and I had no idea what humans wanted—not least one as special and perfect as her.

So, instead, I watched her from a distance, falling for her a little more every day.

Then, suddenly, she was just *gone*. Guess she went back home to wherever she lived.

My beast was destroyed. It almost went insane with anguish. It turned violent, destroying everything in its path. I almost got put down.

But then I had a moment... amid the hell of my madness, I realized—maybe I can become the man this princess deserves.

I gathered the last reserves of my sanity, and got my shit together. I joined the military—a trial program for savage, uncivilized shifters like me—and I learned how to be a human. It was tough, and there were some dark, dark days, but the thought of my mate kept me going. Kept me working on myself.

Four years later, I got out, and I came back here and built this cabin with my own hands. It was meditative, constructive. At last, I've gotten myself civilized. The only thing I didn't do was fix up her cabin. I wanted to have everything perfect for her, and then I was gonna track her down in the spring.

But here she is, right on my doorstep. And there's no way I'm going to let her slip through my fingers this time.

A slight frown creases her soft forehead, and in the sweetest voice I've ever heard, she says, "were you expecting me?"

My breath catches.

You have no idea.

I scan her features hungrily, seeing how she's matured since last time I saw her. Her eyes are the same—huge and bright blue, sparkling from her pale winter complexion. But her lips are plumper now, and the deepest cherry red. She has the same cute, button nose, but her cheeks are a little less rounded, reflecting a grown woman's beauty. Her blonde hair shimmers like spun gold beneath her knitted gray hat, and she's wearing a thick, chunky coat, but I can just make out the ripe curves that lie beneath. I inhale deeply, letting her scent flood my nostrils. Honey, lavender. Some kind of feminine beauty products. Sweet and heady and delicious.

Mine, my animal growls. *Claim her.* It's all stirred up. Pacing and scratching me up inside. Desperate to get to her.

I gaze deep into those cornflower-blue eyes. "Only all of my life," I say.

A shadow of uncertainty passes across her eyes.

Darn, that was too much. She's not used to hearing such things, of course. Not from half-naked strangers, in the middle of nowhere.

I sense she isn't used to trusting people either, but she gives me the benefit of the doubt. She doesn't turn away, step back. Good. I don't want her to doubt a single thing I say to her. Ever.

What happened to her, though? There's something about her—I see it now. The tension in her face, the hunch to her shoulders.

Someone hurt her.

The certainty hits me like a thunderbolt.

Fury charges my veins. I'm gonna find out who it was and destroy them. Make them wish they'd never been born.

But I need to go slow. I need to be careful not to scare her. I put the axe down.

Then I feel it—vibrations beneath my feet. Vehicle tires, heading in this direction.

Goddamn cops.

They're still far away, but I have about two minutes before they show up.

"Only kidding." I force out a laugh, but it sounds dry, grating. Guess I haven't laughed for a while. "Haven't seen anyone at the cabin for a long time."

"Oh." Relief flashes across her face and she laughs, too. A sweet tinkling sound, like summer streams dancing over pebbles.

"I'm sorry to disturb you. I'm Rowan." She thrusts out her hand.

Rowan. What a beautiful name. All these years, I've wondered what it might be.

And *fuck.* Is she really offering me her hand to touch? I take it in my massive paw and grasp it reverently. It's tiny and encased in a woolen glove, but I can feel her warmth flowing through to my own hand. Soon, I'll be feeling *all* her warmth against my body, with no barriers between us.

One of her pale gold eyebrows is raised questioningly. I frown. Did I miss something?

"And you are—?"

Damn, I'm supposed to be telling her my name, like a normal human. "Jaxton," I say.

"Pleased to meet you, Jaxton," she says and laughs again. I love the way my name sounds in her mouth.

When she's mine I'll get her to say it to me over and over.

They're a minute away.

"I've been having a little car trouble," she continues, clasping her hands together. "But I really need to get some reinforcements from Twin Falls before the storm blows in. I was wondering if you'd be willing to give me a ride there?"

She's so hesitant, so apologetic for asking, but my heart is bounding in my chest.

My girl, enclosed in my vehicle. Only inches away from me. Her delicious scent filling the interior. My beast shudders beneath my skin. It's more than I can handle. I swallow hard.

But now she's backing away. "I'm s-sorry, it's too much. I shouldn't have asked—"

"I would love to," I manage to get out.

But first I need to get rid of the cops. They're almost here. I need to get her inside so she doesn't overhear whatever they're going to say to me.

She's staring at me, confused, expectant.

"You want a warm drink before we go?" I ask.

They're driving down the lane leading to the cabins now. I can hear the gravel crunching.

Twenty seconds. I open the back door to the cabin and invite her in.

But she frowns and turns away. Then she heads to the front of the cabin, just as their car comes to a halt.

My heart sinks. They're going to tell her about my brother's latest screw up—whatever it might be. And she's going to run like hell.

I stay in the shadows, ears pricked up.

"Evening, Miss," says a throaty human cop voice. I clench my fists, just imagining how he's looking her up and down.

"Evening," she says politely.

"This is Jaxton Faulkner's place?" says another voice. Thin, reedy.

"I guess so," Rowan replies.

"Is he home?"

There's a half-second pause.

My blood pounds in my veins; my beast prepares to burst out of me.

"No," she says.

I blow out a long breath. She's protecting me? There's no reason why she would do that. Unless—

Mine! my beast roars.

Is it possible she feels the mate connection, too?

"You sure, now?" says the reedy voice again. *Condescending prick.*

"Sure as I can be." She's a little nervous, but she holds firm. Admiration pours through me.

"Jaxton is a dangerous man." The first cop now. "Wouldn't want a pretty little thing like you to get caught up with him."

Liar! My beast swells beneath my skin, and I cage its bellow behind my teeth. I'm gonna tear him to pieces. Make him sorry he ever laid eyes on my girl.

But her next sentences takes my breath away.

"I'll be okay," she says.

My chest warms. She doesn't believe him. If she did, she'd ask what makes me dangerous.

I hear him grunt in disappointment. That wasn't what he wanted to hear. He wanted her to be weak and helpless. Bile rises in my throat. I know humans like him. Trying to force women to be weak so they look strong in comparison. Well, my girl's not taking any of that shit.

"His vehicle's here—" the second cop mutters.

"Can you give me a ride into town?" Rowan cuts in.

She's protecting me, again. I close my eyes, savoring the feeling. She knows she's mine. My mate.

"I'm staying at the next cabin along, but my car's broken down and I need to get a few things to keep the cold out. Looks like it's gonna be a freezing night."

"It'd be my pleasure, ma'am," the first cop says.

My beast bristles. *I* should be the one taking her to town. Buying her whatever she wants. Carrying it all for her. Instead, I'm stuck here, hiding from these assholes.

"Lemme just check he's not holed up inside here," says the second cop.

There's a pause, then the rap of knuckles on my front door. "Can't see him." He's cupping his hands around my window now and peering inside. I can feel it. Then there's the sound of human feet walking along my decking. I dart behind a tree and watch as the uniformed human completes a circuit of my property. It's all I can do to keep my beast inside me.

"Nope. He's not here."

"Let's go."

I listen as they clamber inside the cop car.

"I'm okay, thanks," I hear Rowan say sharply. She's

rejecting his offer of assistance. I smile to myself. I hate the fact that she's alone with these two bozos, but I know she can handle herself.

The moment the vehicle has gone from earshot, my animal unleashes a roar of rage.

Then I snatch up the axe again and get to work double time. Need to make sure my princess has plenty of firewood to heat up her place when she gets back. I'm still mad at myself for not getting her cabin ready in time, but I'll do what I can to make her place as cozy as can be. Then, when she trusts me a little, I'll find out who's hurt her and take them out.

And finally, I'll make her mine.

3

Rowan

a polar sleeping bag, an electric heater, a small bag of firewood and another ride in the police car later, and I'm back at the cabin again.

"You gonna be okay in there by yourself? Looks awful isolated," the sleazy cop—whose name, I've discovered, is Rivers—says.

"Yeah, I'll be fine. I know this place well." I turn to Jaxton's cabin automatically. Weird thing is, if I hadn't met my scary, half-naked neighbor, I might've been nervous staying here alone. But somehow, his presence makes me feel safe.

Am I crazy? *Probably.*

But for some reason, I'm getting much better vibes from an axe-wielding mountain man than this officer of the law.

Rivers hands me something—his card. "You need something to keep you warm later, you let me know—"

"I came here for some peace and quiet," I say pointedly.

He pouts. "Just sayin'."

Out of the corner of my eye, I see the other cop shake his head. I get the impression he's not impressed by his friend's antics. He hauls the bag of firewood out the trunk of the cruiser. "Can I bring this inside for you, ma'am?"

I hesitate. It's too heavy for me to carry by myself, but I don't want them intruding in my little cabin. "Just by the door's fine," I say. He brings the heater, too, and I snatch up the sleeping bag.

"Blizzard's just about here." He tips his head back and looks at the sky. "You be careful now."

"I will. Thanks for your help," I say.

I haul the heater inside and make sure I've slammed the door shut before they've pulled out of the driveway.

I'm grateful they gave me a ride, but I'm glad to see the back of them, Rivers especially.

I shiver as I step into the cabin again. I swear it's even colder than outside. I flick on all the lights and find a place to plug in the electric heater. I don't think it'll make a ton of difference. The wind is howling through a broken windowpane and several gaps in the wood planks. But the sleeping bag is supposed to keep me warm down to zero degrees, and surely it won't get colder than that?

I'll be fine here. This isn't shaping up to be the cozy

weekend of reminiscence I was hoping for. But I'm determined to make the best of it.

When I dash out to get my supplies from the car, an icy gust of snow blasts me in the face.

Okay, the blizzard's here.

I bring everything in, making three trips to get the firewood. I'm trying hard not to let my gaze drift to the other cabin down the road, but it's no use.

Is Jaxton in there right now? Is he still walking around half-naked, apparently oblivious to the cold? A shudder goes through me. I picture snowflakes coating his huge pecs and his incredible, rippling abs. Sizzling as they meet the heat of his body. He's the most gorgeous man I've seen in my entire life. I imagine pressing my face to his skin, running my hands all over him. Him kissing me, caressing my…

Whoa… wash your mind out, young lady! I can feel my cheeks glowing in the cold, like a beacon.

I shut the door, closing out the blizzard—and Jaxton, and turn my attentions to the fireplace. I already researched how to build a fire. Shouldn't be too hard.

I lay out some newspaper and wood and firelighters and get to work.

But five minutes later, and the flames aren't catching like they're supposed to.

Darn. My back is aching and I've wasted a bunch of matches. I sit back on my heels and stare at the dying flame in dismay. What am I missing? Could the chimney be blocked or something—?

There's a loud knock at the door.

Adrenaline darts through me. Has that idiot cop come back?

"Yeah?" I call, without getting up. My throat is tight and my voice sounds scratchy.

"Hey, it's Jaxton," comes a deep rumble. "Just wondering if you needed anything?"

My heart beats fast. I leap to my feet and yank the door open.

There he is.

His huge bulk is filling the doorway. He's wearing a denim shirt now, over a white t-shirt, which outlines his massive pecs. His shirt and dark hair are covered in snowflakes, and he looks sexier than ever. I try not to stare at him too obviously.

"Hi," I manage to say.

He rubs at his beard. "Sorry if I scared you."

"Oh, you didn't." I swipe at my hair, then thumb over my shoulder. "I-I was just getting frustrated with the fire."

He frowns. He's way too dark and brooding for his own good.

"It won't catch? Probably because those logs are a little damp. Here." He steps off to the side of the doorway and when he straightens up again, he's holding a gigantic pile of logs. "Brought you these," he grunts.

Wow.

My scary, indecently sexy neighbor is bringing me firewood?

My whole body lifts.

I restrain a grin of delight and throw the door wide open.

He brings them in and piles them up to the side of the fireplace. "Let's see if we can get this thing going." He tears off his shirt, kneels down and gets to work.

"Can I help?" I ask.

"Nope," he grunts.

Okay, then.

Guess there's nothing else to do but stand here and stare at him unashamedly. I fold my arms and watch the muscles rippling beneath his T-shirt. Those broad shoulders, that powerful back. Thinking thoughts I've never had before. Trying to ignore that tingling in the core of my body.

I feel excited, overwhelmed.

Hungry.

The police said he's dangerous. I must be crazy. But all I can think is how much I want him to touch me.

Too soon for my liking, Jaxton stands up and wipes his hands on his jeans. The fire is glowing in the hearth. "That'll last you all night if you keep piling logs on it."

"Wow, I don't know how to thank you," I say. "Can I offer you a hot drink at least?"

A smile tugs at the corners of his lips. "You're welcome, and only if it's no trouble?"

"No trouble at all," I say, and my heart gives a little jump.

He's staying longer.

I *want* him to stay longer.

Those two thoughts make me dizzy.

While I pull out my travel kettle and fill it with water, he prowls around the cabin, examining the windows. "Any tape in those drawers?" he asks.

"I don't know..." I open Grandma Jo's ancient wooden drawers and root through. They're filled with knickknacks, but at last I find a roll of silver tape. "This any good?"

"Perfect." He snatches it up and gets to work, taping around the edges of the windows. I add hot water and teabags to two earthenware mugs. I remember drinking from them with Grandma, and I kind of like the fact that this sexy-scary mountain man and I are using them now. I watch Jaxton subtly as I finish up. He rips the strips of tape off with his teeth, and before I know it, every single pane has been taped and the broken window has been covered over. He's so capable, so skilled with his hands. And it's so darn sexy.

"Amazing," I say, kind of stunned. "Thanks so much again."

He accepts the mug of tea with a nod. "I'll do a better job tomorrow, but that'll help keep the heat in tonight."

"Oh, you've done more than enough." I say. "You've saved me, truly."

He flashes a grin. "Just returning the favor."

I open my mouth and close it again. I'm dying to ask him why those idiot police were looking for him, but I know it's none of my business.

He takes a sip of his drink, and I watch, captivated, as he raises the mug to his full lips.

"Thank you for what you did back there—" He breaks off, rubs at his beard. "I swear to you, I haven't done anything wrong. Nothing illegal. I just can't explain right now why they're on my case. So, thank you, so much for having my back."

I wave my hand in embarrassment. "Oh, it's nothing—"

"No—" His tone gets extra serious. "It's not nothing. I was a stranger to you, but you chose to protect me against some men with badges. That means a lot."

I blink, unsure how to respond. "I just did what came naturally," I say at last. Which is the truth. I feel like he's a good guy, beneath that scary exterior. And I should know; I've spent a ton of time around bad men. Some of them are my own relations. "Besides, one of them was a real dick."

His jaw juts out and a sound bursts from his lips—a feral, growly sound that belongs more to an animal than a human.

"Huh?" I yelp. "What was that?"

His eyes are blazing with a strange light. "Nothing." He coughs into his fist, shakes his head impatiently. "He didn't do anything to you... try to touch you or something?"

"No, nothing like that."

"Good. He ever bothers you again, you tell me, okay, and I'll deal with him."

I nod cautiously, getting the distinct impression Jaxton is offering to rip his head off for me.

And god knows, I shouldn't like that, but I do. Somehow it connects with a little spot between my thighs, which is already aching like crazy.

He wants to protect me, look out for me. Is that all he wants?

Jaxton leans back against the fireplace and gives me a long, appraising look. "Now, tell me, Rowan. What brings you to this frozen little place in the middle of a blizzard?"

"Uhhh…" A nervous laugh bubbles out of me. Because anything other than the truth is going to sound so ridiculous now.

"I could ask you the same thing," I manage to say, and I'm amazed at how strong and sassy my voice sounds.

He folds his arms. "A fair question, I guess. I live here year-round. I'm used to the elements." He looks me up and down, taking in my clothes. "How about you, city girl?"

I stiffen, imagining he's mocking me. But there's only good-natured teasing in those deep, dark eyes of his.

"I-I needed a vacation. Some time to myself," I say at last.

He frowns. He's not buying it. I hate the way I'm being cagey with him. But I can't tell him the truth. I couldn't stand to see the disgust on his face when he understands what I've agreed to do.

I swallow hard. "This was my Grandma Jo's old cabin. I've been meaning to come back here for years."

That's true at least.

His expression softens. "Were you close to your grandma?"

I nod. My throat is tight and suddenly, I'm close to tears. "I still miss her so much," I get out.

He looks… startled… pained? It's hard to interpret the shift in his expression. "I'm so sorry for her passing," he murmurs.

"Did you ever meet her?"

"A few times," he says. "She was a real special lady."

I kind of laugh and sob at the same time. "She was. I didn't see a lot of her when I was growing up, but the times I spent here with her were some of the happiest days of my life."

A smile tugs at the corners of his lips. "That's what I thought—" He breaks off.

"Huh?"

"Oh, nothing." He shakes his head dismissively.

My heartbeat speeds up. I feel like I've missed something. Something important.

"Did she leave you this place?" he asks.

"She didn't make a will, so it was kind of left to the family. Not that my dad is interested in it—" I break off. My father is the last person I want to talk about right now.

Several emotions pass across Jaxton's eyes. "And your mother?" he says in a low tone, as if he already knows the answer.

"She passed when I was eight."

"You poor thing." His eyes are full of sympathy, and if I don't change the subject now, I might really burst into tears. I'm not used to sympathy. I've always had to be the strong one, for Charlie's sake.

I shrug. "So, I came back to see if the old cabin was still in one piece. Maybe I'll return in the spring, fix it up properly."

His eyes light up. "I can do that for you."

I open my mouth and close it again.

He's offering to work on my place? After this weekend, I'll never see this little cabin again, but I do love the thought that it'll be cared for. Right now, I can't afford to pay him though. I barely have a cent to my name...

"For free, of course," Jaxton says, like he read my mind.

My body jolts.

I'm a complete stranger to him, but he'd make all this effort for me? Am I in the middle of some beautiful, ridiculous dream?

A gust of wind rattles the windows and I jump. "Wow," I mutter.

He works his jaw back and forth. "I don't recommend you sleep here tonight. Look, why don't you stay at my place? It's small, but I can sleep on the couch. The bed's kind of off in an alcove, so you'll have some privacy—"

"No, it's fine," I cut him off. After everything he's done, no way am I going to kick him out of his own bed. Besides, with the burning hot attraction raging through me right now, sleeping in the same room as him would be super awkward. "I've got my sleeping bag. I know how to keep the fire going. I'll be okay."

Those thick, black eyebrows of his tug together. "There's not a lot of reception up here, but I'm giving you my number. You can change your mind at any time. Just call me and I'll come get you."

"Oh, I could walk—" I blurt out stupidly, because I'm all hot and flustered and overwhelmed.

He shakes his head. "Not in this weather. It gets wild out here, like you wouldn't believe." I follow his gaze to the window, and a shiver goes through me. In summer, it felt so peaceful here. I didn't appreciate how high up we are. How exposed to the elements.

I was naïve coming here in the dead of winter, and I'm grateful once again that Jaxton came to my rescue.

He looks around the cabin once more. "Guess I should get going," he says, but he doesn't make a move to leave. Instead, he looks at me, those dark eyes burning with intensity.

He wants me.

He's way out of my league, but I feel it deep in the core of my body. Like a deep, primal part of us is connecting. I want this to happen. In three days' time, my life will be out of my control forever. But right now... here's this incredibly sexy, kind, mysterious man standing in front of me, undressing me with his eyes.

"Kiss me." The words tumble out of my mouth before I can stop them.

Jaxton's eyes narrow.

I freeze.

Crap. What the hell did I just say?

Shame and embarrassment pour over me in a hot tide.

He doesn't want to kiss me. I just made a huge mistake. He's been helping out a neighbor in need, that's all. And now here I am, making things hella awkward.

"I-I-I'm..." I stutter, but the words won't come out. *Dang.* This is the first time I've propositioned a man in my life. And I've totally humiliated myself. Of course, he's not interested in me. He's a grown man, and he probably sees me as a kid. What an embarrassment I am. Making such an ass of myself when this man has been nothing but kind—

Jaxton steps closer, his big arms stretch toward me, and he drags me into his embrace. Raw hunger burns in his eyes. There's no mistaking it this time.

He dips his head. My heart pounds.

And he kisses me.

He *kisses me.*

Those firm, lush lips crush against mine. They're velvet, with the exciting roughness of his stubble grazing my cheek.

Oh, bliss. My eyelids flutter closed.

My first ever kiss.

With this hot mountain man.

He's gentle at first, but then he goes deeper, forcing my lips apart. I have no idea what I'm doing, but instinctively, I tilt my head, and his tongue slides into my mouth. A wild flame of desire lights inside me. I reach my arms around his neck, clinging to him. I want him to take me. I want all of him inside me. My whole body is on fire for this fierce, sexy man. Nothing else is real, nothing else exists, apart from this passion between us.

Possession floods my mind. The thought of being *his.*

He holds me tighter and tighter, his tongue plunging deep, his body pressed against mine. His breathing is rough and growly. Thick with need—

And he tears his mouth away.

I stare at him, lips still parted, too stunned to move.

"Sorry," he mutters. "Got carried away." He takes a step away from me.

I stagger backward, too. Press the back of my hand to my lips. I want to tell him not to apologize. But maybe he didn't mean it like that? Maybe he didn't like kissing me.

It hurts, but I can take it. At least I'll have this moment to cherish forever.

4

Jaxton

My beast is running full pelt, churning up the fresh snow with its massive paws. I've been trying to get rid of my massive boner, but it's no use. There's only one thing that will do that, and she's currently zipped up in a sleeping bag, sleeping sweetly in her grandma's old bed.

Every nerve, every thought is focused on Rowan. I can't believe she's come back into my life. A woman now, and more beautiful than ever. She's everything I knew she would be, and more.

Last night, when she asked me to kiss her, the universe tilted on its axis. There she was, her beautiful face lifted toward me like a flower. Lips pursing, cheeks adorably pink from embarrassment, but resolution burning in those lovely eyes of hers.

All these years, all these lonely nights, I've dreamed of this moment, but I never really believed it could happen.

And when her lips brushed mine for the first time, it was all I could do to keep my beast inside me. My cock surged, as hard as a rock. My beast roared for me to take her. Her sweet, virgin scent filled my nostrils. She's so ripe, so ready. I could have seduced her right there and then. But it was too soon. When you've longed for your mate as I've longed for Rowan all these years, you don't rush these things. You don't take her for the first time in a broken-down cabin. You get the place warm and cozy and romantic, so she doesn't feel even a flicker of cold when you unwrap her body for the first time. Then you lay her down on luxurious sheets, so she feels like the princess she is, and cherishes this moment forever.

My bear runs on and on. It should be exhausted because I spent all night outside her cabin, keeping watch over her. I was worried she might be cold. Worried that sleazy cop might somehow make it through the blizzard to get to her.

Not happening.

She's mine, and I'm never leaving her unprotected again.

The cold was no problem for my beast and its shaggy coat. And there was one little gift—a crack between the curtains beside her bed. Hidden in the darkness, I peered through and watched as she got into the sleeping bag and pulled it all the way up, fastening the hood tightly around her chin. Then she pulled a thick comforter over her as well, until all I could see was her little face, as pure and beautiful as an angel's. I dozed from time to time, resting my beastly head on my paws. But at least every half hour, I awoke and checked on her, seeing her turn from her left side to her right, then onto her back. Her sleepy sighs reaching my ears, filling me with tenderness.

Soon, I promised my beast. It was scrabbling to get at her, of course. Tearing up my skin. It was almost unbearable.

Soon I'll be in her bed, and she'll be in my arms, and nothing will separate us—ever again.

I let her get away once, but now the universe is giving me a second chance and I'm not gonna waste it.

I need to get the truth out of her if it's the last thing I do.

There was such sadness in her voice yesterday. It tore at me. Ripped the guts right out of my body. She's suffering, and this is about more than missing her grandma. I know it deep in my soul.

My girl is tough and independent, but there's something about her that I can't quite put my finger on, though. A kind of desperation. She feels like someone who knows the world is going to end in three days and she's determined to seize the day. But why? She's got her whole life ahead of her.

I have to know what's hurting her. I have to, so I can fix it.

My cabin is in sight now. I've finished a big loop of the mountains, pausing to snatch up a rabbit or two in my jaws. Now I'll go take a shower, then check on

Rowan. She'll probably be waking up soon and she'll be hungry for breakfast. I want to make sure she's well fed.

Yearning roars through my body at the thought of seeing her again.

* * *

I'M JUST TURNING off the shower, when there's a knock at the door. I grab a towel, wrap it around my waist and yank the door open.

There she is. Wrapped up in her big, black winter coat like a gift I can't wait to unwrap.

At the sight of me, her eyes widen. I look down, following her line of vision and realize I still have a bunch of soap on my stomach.

"Oh, sorry about that." I lift up the towel, wipe it off, and her eyes widen some more. *Crap* Did I just give her a flash of my junk? I know humans get freaked out about stuff like that. And now I'm in danger of getting hard again. I just jerked off in the shower, but the sight of her is too much for my bear to handle. "Sorry," I say again.

"N-no, don't worry, it's fine," she stammers, her cheeks flushing.

Warmth blooms in my chest. She's so gorgeous and natural and heavenly. I'm in love with her. Just like I've always been.

I open the door wider. "You want to come in while I get dressed?"

She hesitates on the doorstep. "I just wanted to say thanks for last night—I-I mean, for fixing the place up and the food." Her face is beet red. She's thinking about the kiss again. It's delightful.

"I was going to offer to cook you breakfast, but—you know—I don't have gas." She gives a nervous laugh. Last night she was so mad at herself when she discovered that the oven ran on gas and she hadn't thought to bring a canister.

"You couldn't think of everything," I tell her again.

"Yeah, but that was dumb. It should've occurred to me. Anyway—" She clasps her hands together. "Then I thought I could get donuts from the town, but you know, my car..." She rolls her eyes self-deprecatingly. "So, words are all I've got for you right now."

"Your words are more than enough, Rowan," I say.

She gives a small, shy smile. *Damn*, she's too cute for words. "And I was wondering—you happen to know anything about the timber and the pieces of furniture that are stacked up beside the cabin?"

"Oh, those," I say casually. "I thought you could probably make use of them. I also took a look at your car. It's fine now."

She gasps. "Oh my god, Are you serious? You fixed it?"

I shrug. "Yup. It was just an issue with the starter motor."

"You're a genius," she says.

"It was easy," I mutter. Which is true. But her admiration in her eyes heats me all the way through.

"Come have breakfast at my place." I make it sound like an order. Guess it is. There's no way I'm letting her go hungry.

Her eyes sparkle. "That would be great. As long as I can cook it."

"Deal," I say, my heart swelling with happiness. She didn't come over just to be polite. She wants to be with me. She doesn't regret last night.

"Come in," I say. Too eager, but my beast's energy is pulsing in my veins.

"Kitchen's over there." I point to the little kitchenette in the corner. "I've got a bunch of stuff in the fridge and cupboards."

"Nice place," she exclaims, walking in and looking around. "It's real cozy."

"Thanks," I say. Compared to her place, which has been unoccupied for four years, it is. But it's not as perfect as I want it to be for her. If I'd known she was coming, I would have gone shopping for a bunch of soft furnishings and stuff. Nice feminine touches to make her feel at home.

Rowan unfastens her coat, and I hurry to slip it off her shoulders and hang it up for her. A waft of her scent fills the room, and a fresh burst of desire hits me like a missile. She smells like honeysuckle and cotton candy. So ripe. So ready for mating. She's wearing a pair of tight black pants and a tight olive-green sweater, both of which show off her lush curves to perfection. And damn, my cock is getting even harder. And I'm still almost naked. I hurry towards the bedroom.

"Make yourself at home," I tell her. "I'll be right back."

When I come back, she's at the stove. I pause for a second, taking in the lovely round curves of her ass, the softness of her shoulders as she works away. Then I stride toward her, because I don't want her to think I've been staring at her like a pervert.

There's something beige and kind of round in the pan. I have no idea what it is.

"Looks good," I say cautiously.

She bursts out laughing. "It looks terrible, doesn't it? I thought it would be nice to make pancakes. But I'm not much of a cook. Oatmeal is my specialty."

I break into a grin. She's just too adorable. I love the way she tries her best, and doesn't let setbacks bring her down.

"So happens I love oatmeal. It's my favorite." I reach up to a high shelf and grab an old bag of oatmeal. "Here we go."

She mixes some milk into it, and before long, that wholesome, sweet smell rises.

I help her ladle it out into two bowls and put them on the table. It's good. She cooked it just right. "This is the best oatmeal I've ever had," I say.

She laughs. "I'm sure you're only saying that."

I go still. I want her to know—especially after that bullshit with the cops—that I'm a man of my word.

"Rowan, I'll never tell you anything I don't mean. I need you to know that," I say.

Her big blue eyes widen and she blinks several times. Then a look of understanding comes into them. "I believe you, Jaxton," she says.

"You can trust me," I tell her.

She's silent for a long beat. Finally, she says in a small voice, "—I *think* I can."

My gut tightens.

She's been through a lot. Far too much for her tender years. My instinct is to drag it out of her right now, but I know that's wrong. I'll make her clam up. I need to go slow, be gentle with this angel.

So, instead, I ask her about her life. I want to know every single thing about her. All her dreams for the future. She tells me about the college she attends, her studies. Her friends. When she mentions guys' names, my beast frets and snarls inside me. I want to quiz her, discover whether they're more than friends, but I don't have the right.

"And after college, what do you want to do?" I ask.

"Oh…" She pushes her oatmeal around her bowl. "I don't know. I…?" She trails off.

"Come on. You must have some dreams? Maybe something you don't usually tell anyone about?"

"No, not really—" She blinks fast, and suddenly she's one step away from tears. Dismay lurches through my gut. Whatever has happened to her has stolen any hope for the future? I grind my teeth. I swear, when she's mine that's the first thing I'm gonna fix.

She starts eating fast, and before long, she's scraping her spoon against the side of the empty bowl.

"Seconds?" I say.

"No, I'm super full." She groans and rubs her stomach. Then her face freezes and she bolts upright. "Gosh, I'm sorry! That wasn't very ladylike."

I can't resist grinning, and I'm damned if my boner doesn't return. "You don't need to apologize to me," I say. "I'm a bea—"

Crap. I was a beat away from telling this tiny human that I'm a big ol' grizzly bear. She's definitely not ready to hear *that* yet.

"How about I come do some work on your place now?" I say instead. "It's gonna be five degrees colder tonight, and you'll need the extra warmth."

She'll be in your bed tonight, my bear reminds me.

There's a hint of hesitation in her eyes. Does she have other plans? Does she have a boyfriend coming to stay with her today? Is that what she's been hiding? My bear starts up a roar. I barely have time to cage it behind my teeth.

"I don't want to take up your time," she says.

My chest warms. She's not hiding a boyfriend. She's being her usual selfless self.

I pause, thinking. I need to make it sound like there's something in it for me. Well, apart from the pure paradise of being in her presence. "You'll be doing me a favor, actually. I get real antsy when I'm snowed in."

"Oh—" Her cheeks turn that adorable shade of pink again. "Well, in that case. Yes, please. That would be amazing."

"Great," I say and I can't restrain the grin from spreading across my face.

When I get up to take our bowls to the kitchen, her phone rings. She picks it up, swipes, and horror crosses her face.

Ice shoots down my spine. It's the person who hurt her. I know it is. My beast swells beneath my skin.

I cross to the kitchen and watch as she reads the

message. Her shoulders tense and her thumb works fast as she types something back.

Snatch the phone! my beast growls.

What?! No. You can't act like that. I shove it back down inside me.

"Everything okay?" I spit the words out fast, before I say something way worse.

"Yeah… sorry," she says, but her voice sounds different now. More distant. I clench my jaw. I'm burning to ask her now. Demand to know who's hurting her, and put it right. Some asshole ex-boyfriend? An intense wave of jealousy wells up inside me. I clench the edge of the sink so hard I feel it crack.

I'll tear him apart, limb by limb. Pulverize him.

She stands up and shoves the phone in her back pocket. Her jaw is set bravely, but there's a slight tremble to her hands.

I hate so much that she feels like this. But I need to bide my time, get her to trust me.

And when she's mine, she'll never suffer a moment of distress again.

"Ready when you are!" Her tone is artificially bright. But if that's what she needs, I'll go along with it. I'd go along with anything to make her happy.

As we're leaving, I remember there's a box of donuts in the fridge. "Reinforcements," I tell her, and her eyes light up.

"Wanna share one now?" I ask.

She wrinkles her nose adorably. "Think it'll keep the cold out?"

"Definitely." I grin. I love that she has this silly side

to her. I hand one to her, and while she keeps hold of it, I tear the other half off.

"Two perfect halves," she exclaims, and my heart warms.

It's as corny as hell, but I can't help thinking it's a symbol of the two of us.

5

Rowan

I shouldn't have kissed Jaxton.

Not when the clock is ticking, counting off my last three days of freedom.

And my father can't even leave me alone to enjoy it. He keeps bugging me to call him. I told him there's not enough reception to connect a call—which is true—but it won't keep him off my back for long.

I'm walking behind Jaxton's big, broad figure, stepping in the tire tracks left by his truck earlier this morning. Snow drifts sit waist high on either side of the road, and the wind is whipping up again, but his bulk protects me from the worst of it.

My stomach is churning, and I'm full of guilt for not telling him the whole story of what I'm doing here. He was so kind when I spoke about my grandma, and now I feel like a fraud.

What was I doing asking him to kiss me, when I was promised to another? I feel like we're getting closer by the minute. Heck, I'm already falling for him. But none of this can happen. Because in three days' time, I'm going to drive out of his life, and he's never going to see me again.

The last thing I want to do is tell him the truth. I want to enjoy these last three days with him. Throw caution to the wind. Lose my virginity to him.

But I feel like I'm betraying him. He deserves more than that. A lot more.

My heart sits heavy in my chest.

And I know that when I tell him the truth, he'll leave.

I walk fast to catch him up, already fumbling for the key in my pocket.

"Jaxton…" I push open the door and as soon as we're both inside the cabin, I turn to face him. I open my mouth, but the words won't come.

The good-natured curiosity on his face kills me.

"I've got something to tell you," I rush out.

He frowns, worry shadowing his handsome features. "What is it, Rowan? Are you sick or something?"

I shake my head, swallow hard.

"The reason why I came here is because in three days' time, I… I'm—"

Darn. How to explain what my father has done to me to a normal person?

"Take your time." Jaxton reaches out and squeezes my shoulder with his massive paw. I almost knock his hand away. It's too much. He's so kind, and I don't deserve it, one bit.

"I'm going to be married—" I blurt out at last.

Not strictly true. Who knows whether my new owner will want to legally marry me, or just keep me as his property?

"Married?" Jaxton's handsome face fills with horror. "B-but… we kissed. You wanted me to kiss you—"

Oh, god. Now he thinks I'm a cheater as well.

He turns on his heel and shoves the door open. "I've got to go," he mutters, stumbling outside.

"Jaxton, please—" I cry. But he doesn't stop.

Shit.

My throat convulses as I watch him stride down the snowy path.

I can't let him think of me like this. I can't stand it.

I rush after him, tripping over my feet.

"My father sold me!" I wail.

"What?" He spins around.

"He's in debt. A lot of debt, to one particular creditor. He was going to go bankrupt, but instead, the creditor accepted me in lieu of the money."

He goes still, then he shakes his head, like my words are too ugly and awkward to fit inside them. I don't blame him. "Accepted you?" he repeats.

"As a… a partner," I say lamely. For his sake, I'm trying to make it sound less awful than it is.

His face fills with disgust, and I flinch.

"I'm s-sorry. I know this is probably a gross thing to hear—"

My words are drowned out by a roar. A sound that

doesn't belong to a human. An earth-shattering bellow. Jaxton's face is changing. His jaw and cheekbones are broadening, somehow. His body is swelling. I goggle at him as his clothes split open.

Underneath is dark-brown fur.

What the—?

Then he turns a one-eighty and *runs.*

I blink fast, unable to believe what I'm seeing.

The hot, sexy human has disappeared, and in his place, is a huge grizzly bear?

Is this really what's happened? But that's impossible…

Shifter.

The word shudders through me.

This is shifter country. The fabled half-man, half-beasts who roam around, hidden from human eyes.

Grandma Jo used to tell me stories about them. About their packs and clans. Their family loyalties. How they mate for life, have a ton of cubs. There was always a wistfulness in her voice when she spoke about them. She said they were real. Not a myth, as most people thought.

And now I find out that Jaxton is one of them?!

The thought is too much for my head to contain. I sink down onto my knees in the snow.

Well, it figures. His huge size. That intense glow to his eyes. The way he was chopping wood half-naked yesterday, even though it was freezing cold.

I shiver. *I kissed a shifter.*

Heat floods to my core.

And I liked it.

I liked it a lot.

I wanted more. I wanted him to mate me.

I wanted him to take my virginity with his big, shifter cock.

But now I've told him about what my father has done and he couldn't get away from me fast enough.

He even left his clothes behind in the process.

I trudge through the snow, to where his shirt is lying. The buttons have burst off of it, and the sleeves are all torn. His T-shirt is ripped down the center. His jeans are all ripped around the waist. And... that's it. There's no underwear to be seen. He goes commando?

Fuck, that's sexy. My mind drifts back to that moment earlier this morning, when he lifted up his towel and showed me... My clit gives a little jump.

Well, that's not going to happen again.

I gather everything up, and because I don't know what else to do, I bring it back to the cabin. Guess none of it is salvageable, and guess I won't see him again anyway, but I find a clothes rack and hang it up to dry.

The fire has almost gone out. I pile a couple more logs on, then I sit on Grandma Jo's old tapestry rug, arms wrapped around my knees, staring deep into the glowing embers.

My heart hurts.

Now the shock of discovering Jaxton's shifter nature is wearing off, I'm aware of this deep pain, taking hold of my body.

Jaxton is such a great guy.

I so wish things had been different. I wish I was just a regular girl who'd decided to come here on a whim.

Single, untainted by my family, and I just happened to run into him.

I wish I was good enough to be Jaxton's partner.

But I'm not. I'm screwed up. That look of disgust on his face is burned into my brain. He doesn't understand such grubby things. Why would he?

I just hope like hell that I haven't hurt him.

6

Rowan

I don't know how much time passes, but I become aware that it's hella dark in the cabin and the wind has gotten even worse.

I snap out of my misery.

I've got to apologize to him. If it's the last thing I do. I grab my phone.

There's no reception, at all.

I look out at the snowdrifts outside. It looks wild out there. But I'll be quick. I'll run all the way.

I grab my coat, fasten it up and brace myself as I open the door.

Yikes.

The wind tears the door from my grasp. It's at least twice as strong as I expected. It blows me against the door frame.

But I'm not going to quit. I brace myself and take off at a run, through the tire tracks. The fresh snow has covered them, though. I stumble and go down. When I stand up, fast-falling snow is driving toward me at an angle, blasting me in the face. Suddenly, all I can see is white. I'm disoriented, and I can't see Jaxton's place at all.

But there's my place, off to my left. I just need to head off in the opposite direction.

Shit. I can hardly stay on my feet. I should go back. But I think I'm almost there. *What if he's not home though?*

I can't think about that now.

Whump. The wind knocks me off my feet, and I tumble into a snow drift. My cheeks are stinging from the cold, and I'm kind of crying from the shock. I stand up... and get knocked down again.

Crap. I need to get back. This is dangerous. Where's my cabin though? The snow is coming so thick and fast. It's a whiteout.

I stagger in the direction I think it's in. But my foot disappears into deep snow, and I'm half buried. I haul myself up, but I'm getting tired. I'm not going to make it—

"Rowan!" a deep voice calls.

Jaxton! My soul cries out to him.

Suddenly, I'm being lifted off my feet. Something warm and solid is surrounding me, blocking out the cold.

Then I'm in Jaxton's truck. The door slams and the wind quits howling.

"You found me." I stare at him in shock.

His face is drawn with worry. "What on earth were you doing out there?"

"I was coming to tell you I'm sorry."

His dark eyes widen. "*You're* sorry? What for?"

"F-for asking you to kiss me when I wasn't available."

He shakes his head. "That kiss was… well, the best darn thing that's ever happened to me. You don't need to apologize for it. Ever." His voice is fierce, and it floods my body with heat.

"But I should've been honest with you."

He frowns. "Why weren't you?"

I bite my lip. "Because I'm so ashamed, I can hardly stand it—"

"No." His big head swings back and forth. "You have nothing to be ashamed of. Your father is the one who should be ashamed, for giving you away like you're his property, and the creditor for thinking it's okay to take you—but let's get you inside. You're freezing."

I nod wordlessly. My head is spinning.

He doesn't hate me? I didn't hurt him?

The truck slides and slides in the soft, deep snow, and it takes a hell of a long time to cover the tiny distance, but at last, we're there, right in front of Grandma Jo's front door. Jaxton darts around to the passenger side and helps me out. The wind is brutal, and the short walk to the front door makes me cold all over again.

I throw the door open wide, but Jaxton hesitates on the doorstep. "You want me to come in?"

"Of course!"

"But... what you saw back there..."

"I know about shifters," I say. It's what he needs to hear right now. I sense it in my soul.

His forehead furrows. "You do?"

"Yup. My grandma told me all about them when I was here last."

"Did you know about... me?"

I shrug. "When I saw you shifting, it all made sense."

His frown deepens. "Are you weirded out to know that you kissed a shifter?"

My heart melts to see this big, fierce man so vulnerable.

"Not at all." I shake my head, and tears prickle at the back of my eyes. "You're the best man I've met. Hands down."

He lets out a deep growly sound of relief. He takes a step into the house, and another one, and closes the door behind him. Then he takes both my hands in his. "You're not going back home, you hear me? You're staying right here with me."

I shake my head. "I can't."

He lets off a snarl. "The hell you can't. I'll protect you, from anyone and everyone."

"I have a little sister," I tell him. "My father's creditor has promised to spare her." I hang my head. "There's a lot of money at stake. He said dad's lucky he's not taking both of us. But if I go willingly, he'll leave Charlie alone. He'll even fund her place at a private school, so my dad can't use her as collateral in future."

"So, you came here for a vacation before you go to live with this… this *person?*" he spits the word out.

"Yup. I did a deal with my father. Four days of peace. And of course, this is where I wanted to spend it. I felt like Grandma Jo's place was calling to me."

"Protecting you," he says in an undertone.

I nod. "I understand if you don't want to have anything to do with me. And I'm so sorry I didn't tell you the truth—"

"Rowan—" His voice is fierce again. "You didn't do anything wrong. You should never have been put in this situation. You're not *with* this person."

"I'm not. I'm single. But in three days' time, I won't be."

"In three days' time." He puts his arms around me and sweeps me right off my feet. Automatically, I wrap my legs around his waist. God, he feels so *right*. Like we fit together perfectly.

"But not now." He presses a kiss to the side of my neck. And another one on my jaw. "Right now, you're free."

"I am," I agree.

He inhales, sniffing me, and makes a sexy sound of pleasure. His lips are getting closer and closer to my own, his stubble brushing my cheek. I feel lightheaded. I'm losing myself in him—

I want this so much. But I'm as confused as hell.

"You don't care that this… this can't last?" I blurt out.

His eyes flash with something… something dark and intense, then they soften again. "Rowan, you're the most amazing person I've met—"

I choke out a laugh. "I don't feel so amazing right now. I feel kind of gross. Not worthy of you."

He jerks backward, like he's been bitten. "Are you kidding?" He cups my face in his massive hands and gazes deep into my eyes. "You're so strong. This thing you're doing—sacrificing yourself like this for your sister… it's beyond brave."

"She's a real good kid," I mutter.

"Even so. This takes real guts, real strength of spirit. The way you didn't take any shit from those cops impressed the heck out of me. But this, this is on another level."

"Really?" I'd never seen myself that way before.

He nods. "Big time. I don't agree with what you're going to do, but you're a grown woman and it's your decision. And in the meantime, I'm gonna make sure the next three days are as happy as they can be."

Those chocolate-brown eyes of his keep staring into my own, and I swallow hard to choke down a sob. He wants nothing more than to make me happy? He's a dream. The perfect guy. I don't want three days with Jaxton. I want a lifetime.

"So?" He shakes his head questioningly.

"What?"

"What do you want to do? Your wish is my command."

I puff out a breath and pull myself together. Okay, I've got this. I'll never be Jaxton's wife, and I can't pretend that doesn't hurt like hell. But I'd be crazy to waste this time with him.

My vision is blurry as I scan the interior of

Grandma Jo's cabin. "I-I guess I'd like to get this place in good shape. I might never see it again, but it'll make me happy to know it's still here, preserving her memory."

He flashes a smile. "We can do that. What else?"

My eyes dart to those firm, masculine lips. "I-I'd really like you to kiss me again."

His smile gets broader. "Done." He leans in, and those firm lips crush against mine again.

I close my eyes and fall, fall into the lushness of his mouth. The bliss of his big strong arms wrapping around me. My whole body lights up, like stars are trailing through it. When I tangle my hands in his hair, he growls and holds me tighter.

His hands slide beneath my sweater, moving higher and higher. And I feel him, his cock, pushing between my thighs. God, that feels good. I'm aching for him. I'm a little nervous, but so ready for him to take me. To make me his—

My phone buzzes.

He groans and puts me down. "Is it him?" he growls.

I retrieve my phone from my back pocket. A dart of alarm goes through me. "No, it's my sister. I have to take this."

There's one bar of signal. I stay still, willing it not to disappear.

"Hey, Charl. Are you okay?" I say, my anxiety already building. She said she wouldn't call unless it was an emergency.

"Why have you been ignoring my calls and my messages?!" a deep voice bellows.

My gut tightens. Not Charlie, but my father, of course.

"I've been trying to relax and enjoy this weekend, Dad—"

"Don't be a smartass. There's been a change of plan," he barks. "I need you back here on Sunday instead of Monday."

"B-but, we agreed—"

Silence greets me on the other end. He's hung up on me. Again.

Noo. My heart plummets. This time with Jaxton is short enough, without losing a day. Throat convulsing, I turn and look for him.

He's pacing up and down, and I can sense his animal, just below the surface. His head snaps toward me.

"Jaxton, I have to—" I break off. Everything is so perfect right now. Here with him in this little microcosm. I can't stand to spoil it.

He takes a step toward me, face taut with anger. "Your father's bullying you to come back early?"

"Yes," I admit. "He took Charlie's phone, because he knew I'd only answer her call."

A growly, snorty sound bursts out of him. "Give me the phone."

"W-why?"

"So I can give him a piece of my mind."

I gulp. As much as I'd love for Jaxton to speak to my father, who knows what effect it'll have on him. To my knowledge, no one's ever stood up to him before.

"Let me deal with him, Rowan," he says in a softer tone.

I close my eyes and something burns in my chest. Something bright and new and real.

I pick up my phone again and dial Charlie's number.

"Yeah?" comes my father's familiar sound of choked rage.

"Please don't cut me off when I'm speaking to you. It's very disrespectful. And I'll be back no Monday night, as agreed."

Before he can reply, I end the call and turn my phone off.

And a huge weight lifts from me.

7

Jaxton

My first instinct is to throw my arms around my beautiful, brave girl. But instead, I give her some space while I keep hauling things into the cabin. She's perched on the back of an armchair, staring out of the window and muttering to herself. I can tell that what she just did was big.

She's never stood up to her father before—that asshole, who thinks he's going to sell her like a used car. Because he's used her love for her sister to manipulate her into doing whatever the hell he wants. I clench my jaw, tense my muscles to keep my animal from breaking through my skin.

I'm so mad right now, but so glad I've gotten the truth out of her. This poor sweet girl. So brave, so self-sacrificing. Even more of an angel than I realized.

Twenty years old and she thinks her freedom is going to end in three days.

Over my dead body.

There's no way in hell I'm going to let her go back home and be sold off to this prick. I'll protect her with my last breath.

But I can't tell her that right now.

Because I know if I do, she'll run. Her protective instinct for her sister is stronger than anything else. And that's a beautiful thing. But she needs to understand that she doesn't need to do everything herself, now. She's got me.

Teaching her this will take time though, and luckily I've got three days to get her to understand that I know what's best for her.

I go out again and grab the final armful of timber. When I come back, she's crouching in front of the fire, building it up again. I stand still for a moment, watching her in admiration. Her delicate looks are a real contrast to her spirit. She's so tough; the equal of any shifter.

I lay out the timber and decide what's gonna go where, and then I get to work, sawing and hammering.

"I'll be your assistant," Rowan calls. "Just give me jobs to do."

I turn my head and look for her. She's done stoking up the fire, and she's standing in front of it, warming her hands. She's so beautiful, so sexy and perfect. I want to toss all these jobs aside and drag her to bed. Impregnate her, so there'll be no question she belongs to me. My cock hardens at the thought. My cub growing in her belly. Tying us together—

But I also want to fix up this place for her.

"You don't have to do anything," I say with a grin.

"I want to. For grandma."

My gut clenches. Poor thing. To have lost her mom *and* her grandma. No family members left to take care of her. I'll do anything I can to help her honor their memories.

"Okay, you got it," I say.

* * *

Rowan

THE BLIZZARD IS HOWLING OUTSIDE, but I feel so safe in this little cabin with Jaxton. Protected from the whole world.

For two hours, we work together in harmony. I feel like I'm an assistant to a master craftsman. He seems to know instinctively how to fix everything, and all the pieces of timber are sawed to the exact dimensions. And all I can do is hand him the things he asks for and watch in admiration.

When we're about done, I go make us some tea.

"How do you do that?" I ask, handing a mug to him.

"Do what?" He wipes perspiration from his brow with the back of his hand, and fixes me with a sexy stare.

"Measure everything so perfectly without using a tape measure."

"Oh." He grins. "It's easy for us shifters. I worked as an engineer in the military. I didn't have any specific training, but when my superiors realized I had this ability, they just about fell over themselves to recruit me to their division."

"You were in the military?" I echo.

"Yup." He straightens up. "For a while anyway. To tell you the truth, I spent most of my formative years in my animal form."

My mouth falls open. "No way?" He's so intelligent, intuitive and handsome. More human than any man I've met before. But I'm still getting used to the fact that he also has this exciting, beastly side.

He takes a deep breath, like he's wondering whether to tell me something.

"Someone hurt you," I blurt out. I don't know where that came from. It just felt right.

He stiffens. I hit a nerve.

He nods slowly. "My dad used to be a detective for the human police force." He leans back against the fireplace, folding his arms. "Until one day, he was shot in the head during a gas station robbery. The doctors saved his life, but after that, he started having blackouts and violent mood swings. My brother and I used to stay in our bear forms to avoid the worst of it. But the problem was, I wound up being more animal than human."

"I'm so sorry, Jaxton—" I start to say, but he holds his hand up.

"Two weeks before I left for the military, I saw you in the forest."

My heart jolts. "You did?"

You were still a kid—"

"I must've been sixteen," I cut in.

A soft look comes over him. "You were so beautiful. I was mesmerized. I wanted to speak to you, but I was worried I'd scare the hell out of you, me being all beastly. And then you were gone.

"That was when I decided I needed to reclaim my human side. So, I found out about this trial program in the military for shifters. I got myself enrolled. I was there for four years. I only just got out a couple of months ago, actually. I hoped you'd be living in this little cabin, of course. But I learned that Jolene had died and you weren't there anymore."

My head is spinning, trying to absorb everything he's saying.

He *liked* me, way back when? He went into the military *because* of me?

"When you arrived at my place yesterday, I couldn't believe it," he continues. "Here in the dead of winter. Like a vision. A snow princess."

My heart is beating fast, and I remember the first word he said to me yesterday.

Finally.

Has he been waiting for me all this time?

No, not possible.

"I wish I'd seen you then," I say.

He shakes his head. "I wasn't good enough for you in those days, Rowan. I was too wild. I could barely speak in full sentences."

An intense look passes across his face. "Remember

that day in the forest—? You were picking berries, putting them in a basket. But something scared you, and you dropped the basket and ran like hell—"

I give a little gasp.

A rustle of leaves, twigs breaking underfoot. The hairs on the back of my neck standing on end.

"Yes, I do—"

"Some creepy guy was following you. But I chased him off. Made sure he never thought about coming after you again."

"Oh, my god. I remember I was real scared. But when I got home, I felt silly, like I'd overreacted. So, I went back and got the basket. And everything felt calm. I felt safe. After that, it was just a perfect time. Just me and my grandma together." I step closer to him. "And you protecting me."

He nods. "After that, I watched you every day—" He breaks off, a frown creasing his forehead. "Not like some kind of creeper."

I lay my hand on his. "I understand. You were keeping me safe."

"I was. I wanted you to enjoy that happy time without worrying about anything."

I close my eyes. "Thank you. It was the best gift you could've given me."

When I open them again, he looks troubled, like he wants to say a lot more.

"What is it?"

He goes still, then he laughs. "It's crazy how you do that."

"Do what?"

"Pick up on my feelings. Guys in the military used to say I was impossible to read. I thought it was because my body language isn't human, but you seem to know exactly what I'm thinking."

I grin. "Guess we have a few things in common."

He gazes deep into my eyes. "Do you feel it?"

"The connection between us?" I hardly know what I'm saying, but it feels right. I feel like Jaxton is the man I was supposed to be with. Like there was a plan for it, set out in the stars, before we even saw each other for the first time.

"You're my mate, Rowan."

My breath catches. *Mate.* That exciting word. Shifters don't just marry, they have mates.

Suddenly, Grandma Jo's words float back across the years.

They're luckier than most of us. They mate for life.

My heart blooms, and I long to be his. To spend my life with him and live among his people and have a ton of cubs.

But it can't be. Because I'm not free. "But I can't stay."

He shakes his head. "Doesn't matter. You'll always be mine. Always were, always will be."

My lip trembles. "But in three days' time, you'll never see me again."

"That doesn't change anything. When a shifter finds its mate, that's it."

"B-but—"

He reaches for me, drawing me to him. "I want to be your first, Rowan," he murmurs, his voice low and growly.

I gasp. "How do you know—?"

"Trust me, I know."

I wrinkle my nose. "You can smell it on me, right?"

He groans. "That sweet virgin scent. It's been driving my beast crazy ever since you arrived."

Oh, god. A squirm of embarrassment goes through me, but it's a kind of pleasurable sensation. Jaxton knows I've never been touched by a man before, and he wants to take my virginity. He wants to see me naked. Wants to push that big cock of his inside me. I give a little shiver.

He frowns. "Is that weird to hear?"

"No, it's kind of sexy, actually," I say, and I press my thighs together, because my pussy is aching like crazy.

A low growl escapes his lips, and he dips his head and kisses me.

He's rougher, hungrier this time. His hands run all over my body, grasping my hips, squeezing my tits through my shirt, while he covers my neck in burning kisses.

"I want you so bad, Rowan," he groans, his lips rough on my skin. "You have no idea." I glimpse his cock, straining at the zipper of his jeans, and I long to touch it.

"So take me," I murmur.

He cups my face and stares deep into my eyes. "I want it to be perfect for you."

"It is. Right here, right now, in this little cabin."

He draws back and scans the room with a frown. "It's not perfect yet. But give me five minutes, okay?"

"Okay," I say, smiling into his mouth as he kisses me again.

Keeping his lips on mine, he backs me up, all the way across the room. When I feel Grandma Jo's old window seat against my calves, I sit down.

"I want you to stay right here, until I come get you," he says.

I nod obediently, appreciating the bossiness of his tone.

Then he pulls the curtain around me. It's not tight to the window, but instead it closes off the little nook from the rest of the cabin. Grandma Jo loved to read here. She used to say that she felt like she was out in nature, even on the coldest of days.

I lean back on the soft cushions and snuggle into the nook, looking out at the snow. It's brutal outside. Already dark, with heavy sleet falling. But on the other side of the curtain, it's all cozy and warm—thanks to Jaxton's expert craftsmanship. I strain my ears and listen to him moving around. The heavy sound of his boots on the floor. Things being lifted up and put back down.

I'm about to have sex with him.

He's going to take my virginity.

We're going to be connected, forever, in a way that no one else can destroy.

I'm as nervous as hell.

But I also want this more than I've wanted anything in my life.

8

Jaxton

$\mathcal{I}$ connect a brand-new gas canister to the oven in the kitchenette. Then I straighten up and survey the cabin.

I've smoothed out the comforter and added some extra pillows to the bed, and it looks cozy and welcoming. I've put a new lightbulb in the bedside lamp, which casts the whole area in a soft glow. I've also lit a bunch of candles. The fire is roaring and the electric heater is chasing the cold from the corners.

A cabin fit for a queen?

I sure hope so. I glance at the nook, where Rowan is concealed behind the curtains, and my cock turns even harder.

I've wanted to make her mine for years. Not going after her, breaking out of the military and hunting her down, cost me every bit of willpower I had. But I was a beast. And she deserved much better than that.

The way she's looking at me now, though—this thing between this is real. I know she feels it, too, and that she wants it as much as I do. And whatever my queen wishes is my command. I'm going to do everything in my power to show her that we belong together.

She's mine. I'll protect her with my life. I'll take down anyone who might want to hurt her.

But first, I'm going to claim her.

The honeysuckle scent of her arousal has been driving my animal insane. She's so ripe, so ready.

But I'm not a beast anymore. I've gotten my animal under control these days. And I want her first time to be perfect.

I take one more look around the cabin to check that everything looks good, and then I stride toward the nook, my cock straining beneath my zipper.

My beast swells in me; my breath vibrates in my chest. Every thought is focused on my mate behind the curtain. My sweet virgin mate.

I mean to be gentle, to go slow with her. But instead I yank back the curtain.

And, at the sight that greets me, a growl of lust bursts from my lips.

* * *

MY GIRL IS STILL CURLED up in the nook, just as I left her. But now she's wearing nothing but her underwear.

She's stripped down to a black bra and black lacy panties.

Fuck. She's absolutely gorgeous. Even more beautiful than I dreamed. And I've dreamed of her naked a lot, believe me. Big round tits, a soft tummy, and lush, creamy thighs.

My beast shoves its way up. My cock is so hard it hurts.

There's a small, embarrassed smile on her face, but her eyes are bright with desire.

"Rowan, so goddamn beautiful," I growl.

She flashes her lovely white teeth. "Really?" she whispers.

"You're a goddess. The most beautiful woman in the world."

"No—" she starts to say, but I dart forward and stop her mouth with a kiss. She's reclining, but now I draw her up to meet me. And for the first time ever, I touch her bare skin. Warm and soft, like velvet. I run my hands over the lovely curve of her waist, her stomach. When I cup her tits through her bra, she gives a little sigh.

She's *sensitive*.

My cock surges again. I unfasten her bra and slide it off slowly, reverently. Her tits emerge, exposed to my gaze for the first time. Big and round, with lovely, caramel nipples. "God, Rowan, you're so sexy."

I cup them in my rough hands. Hands that are too coarse to touch this angel, but a ragged moan breaks from her lips.

I lean in and take one of those tender candies into my mouth.

She sighs and moans as I lick and suck on them, her nails digging in to the base of my neck, directing me.

The scent of her desire rises up, sweet and heady. She's ready. I think about taking her right here on the window seat. Tearing her panties aside and plunging my cock into her.

But, no, her first time will be on the bed, in comfort. I'm gonna go slow, give her a night she'll never forget. Besides, I don't want to risk anyone getting a glimpse of her lovely body. It's for my eyes only.

I lift her up into my arms, and she wraps her legs around my waist, just like she did before. But this time there's only a little scrap of fabric between me and her sweet pussy. In a few minutes there'll be nothing between us.

The thought roars in my blood. All these years I've fantasized about her. All those lonely nights when I've laid in bed alone, jerking off, thinking about mating her. Now here she is, wrapped around me, in just her lingerie.

Her lips clings to mine, hungrily. When I slide my tongue into her mouth, she sucks on it a little, welcoming me in. *Fuck.* I imagine how her pussy is going to feel wrapped around my cock, squeezing it.

I walk over to the bed and lay her down.

Finally, she looks around the room, and gives a little gasp. "Jaxton! This is beautiful."

"You like it?"

"Yeah, I love the way you've made it… different. This is *ours*."

My chest warms as I pick up her meaning. This is still Grandma Jo's cabin. And it will always be. But now it's ours, as well. We've put our own mark on it.

I reach for her again, but she shoves me back playfully. "Come on, Jaxton," she says, her eyes shining with a mixture of mischief and desire. "Let me see that body of yours again."

My beast lets out a rumble of delight. She doesn't need to tell me twice. Like all shifters, I feel most in my element when I'm naked. I tear off my shirt, followed by my jeans.

And she kneels back on the bed, and *looks*.

Damn, she looks like a pinup model. But hotter than any model I could imagine. I love the way her hair curls so prettily around her shoulders. The way her tits thrust up toward me. And the way her sweet, soft thighs are spread a little, and I can just make out a patch of dampness on her underwear. She's wet. *For me?* For a big ol' rough-ass bear like me? I still can't believe it.

Her eyes rake me up and down, before zoning in on my cock. Out of the corner of my eye, I can see it jutting out like a tree branch, and I swear it swells even more under her attentions.

"So big," she murmurs.

"I'll go slow," I tell her. Hardly knowing what I'm doing, I encircle my shaft and give it a couple of slow strokes.

"Is it gonna fit inside me?" She sounds adorably

doubtful, and I jerk my hand away. I'm in danger of coming before I've even touched her.

"I just want to make you feel good, honey," I tell her. "I'm only gonna mate you when you're ready."

Emotions flicker across her beautiful blue eyes—excitement, nerves and need.

"Oh, I'm ready for you, Jaxton," she says. "Can I—?"

I hold my breath as her small, soft hand rises up and encircles my cock.

"Oh, it's so hard," she says. I grunt through gritted teeth.

"I've never—" She doesn't finish the sentence. *She's never touched a cock before.*

Delicious. She's completely inexperienced. Her soft hand keeps exploring. Running up and down the length of my cock, then gently cupping my balls. She might have never touched a man before, but she seems to know exactly how to pleasure me.

"Rowan—" I snatch her hand away.

Alarm darts across her features. "You don't like it? Did I make a mistake?"

I shake my head. "You couldn't make a mistake if you tried. I just can't hold back."

"Oh." She giggles, her cheeks pink.

"You have any idea how much I want you, Rowan? How long I've dreamed of this moment?"

"You have?"

"Like you wouldn't believe. Every single day, since I saw you last."

She gives a little moan.

Damn, those sexy little sounds of need. My cock pulses again.

"You've imagined doing this with me?"

"Yup. But I'll tell you what—it's nothing compared with the reality."

When I reach for her panties, she doesn't stop me. I hook my fingers into the sides and peel them off.

She's even wetter than I realized. They're drenched.

As for her pussy... my beast purrs as I see it for the first time. So pink and perfect, already slick with her wetness.

Impatiently, I tear her panties all the way off and spread her wide.

"Oh!" she yelps.

"Let me see, honey," I growl.

She lifts a hand to her mouth, but she doesn't stop me as I hold her thighs apart and take her in. Such a pretty little pussy. I spread her pink lips, devouring the sight of her virgin entrance.

Mine, my beast growls.

Then I dip my head and taste her for the first time.

She tastes just as good as she smells. Sweet cotton candy. When I flick my tongue over her clit, her hips jolt. She whispers my name, *Jaxton, Jaxton*, just like I dreamed she would.

It's all the encouragement I need.

I dive right in.

I lick her all over, plunging my tongue as far inside her as I can. She's so small, so tight. untouched.

Then I fasten onto her clit.

"Oh, that feels good," she breathes. "So good."

I lick and lick her little bud. Before long, she's getting close. She reaches down and tugs on my hair. I fucking love it. My girl's turned into a fierce, wild, sex goddess.

She trembles like a volcano threatening to blow—

When she finally erupts, it's the sweetest thing I've heard in my life. Gasping, panting, sighing, while her honey flows over my tongue.

"Don't stop," she whispers, and I keep going until, finally, the tremors ebb away, and she collapses exhausted on the comforter.

When I lift my head, I see she's laid her elbow across her eyes.

"So that's what a climax feels like," she says.

I grin. She's never even touched herself before. I'm so glad I was the first one to give her an orgasm.

"I hope it was a good one."

"Oh it was the best, trust me." She giggles.

I draw back and take her in. What a sight. Reclining against the pillows, her beautiful body all spread out from me... and her gaze fixated on my cock.

She bites her lip. "Is it... Will it hurt?" she asks in a small voice.

"Maybe for a second," I say. "But then it'll start to feel real good." God knows I don't want to hurt her. "We're going to go real slow," I tell her. "Make sure it feels real good for you."

"I'm sorry," she says. "I probably sound ridiculous. It's just that I've never—"

"Me neither."

Her eyes get huge. "You… You've never had sex before? Are you kidding me?"

I laugh. "As soon as I laid eyes on you that day, four years ago, I was a goner. I've never had eyes for another woman."

She gives me a small, incredulous smile. "Are you serious?"

I nod.

"What if you never saw me again?"

I shrug. "Wouldn't matter. You're my mate. My bear made its claim on you. I knew that day, if I hadn't found you again, I would've just lived the rest of my life alone and celibate."

"Oh, Jaxton, that's beautiful," she says. And then she cries out a louder, *Oh!*

Because all this time, I've been making my way up the bed, sliding in between her thighs, and now the tip of my cock is pressing against her tiny pussy. I ease out, then slide in a little bit. She cries out again and grabs my shoulders.

"Too much?" I ask.

"No." Her beautiful eyes grow fierce. "Just take me, Jaxton. Just fuck me like you want to. Mate me. Make me yours. I don't want you to hold back. I want you to be the big fierce shifter you are."

My animal surges beneath my skin. It's rough, feral, and it wants nothing more than to claim her savagely. But I'm not a beast anymore. I've worked hard to become a man who deserves her, and the human in me fights back.

I go slow, sliding into her, inch by inch, letting her get used to my girth.

She pants and gasps. She's so small, so tight, but finally, my cock tears through her virginity and fills her all the way up.

She gives a wild cry. "You're inside me," she gasps.

"Did I hurt you?"

She shakes her head no, but I can feel the tension in the thighs that cling to my hips.

"Just claim me Jaxton," she cries, her breath sweet and hot in my ear.

I slide my cock out halfway and back in again.

She moans. "That feels *good*."

"Yeah," I agree. Which might be the biggest under-statement in the universe. My girl's sweet virgin pussy clinging to my cock for the first time ever. Those tiny muscles clenching around me. Hot and wet and slippery.

I pump in and out a couple of times. "Oh—" she says in a different voice. "That's like before... I'm going to..."

I thrust one-two-three more times, and she *explodes*. She comes all over my cock, clenching and shuddering and sighing and moaning. I watch as my beautiful girl comes apart in my arms, my cock almost splitting her in two.

She's mine, I think, over and over. Always has been. Always will be. If I never touched her again, I could die a happy man. But that's not gonna happen. Because she's my mate, and I'm going to spend the rest of my life making her as happy as she deserves to be.

Her orgasm has died away, but she's still clenched in

a vise grip around my cock. As I push into her sweet body, again and again, I feel like she's milking me. I'm getting close. My beast is surging to the surface. My jaw aches as its canines push through.

Flip her. Claim her, it growls.

I can't right now.

But already, I'm raising her lovely thighs and turning her onto her side. I'm not going to claim her. I'm just going to mate her from behind. I draw her into my arms, her round ass pressing into my hips as I thrust in this new position.

She makes a sound of surprise and pleasure.

Claim her, my beast rumbles over and over. I clench my jaw, force it back, back.

It's not time yet.

I hold her tight, grasping her full tits as I plough into her, over and over.

And finally, a roar breaks from my throat and I ejaculate inside her. She arches and writhes as I flood her womb with my hot seed. I'm dimly aware that we're coming at the same time, and it's so goddamn beautiful.

9

Rowan

$\mathcal{I}$'m sitting at Grandma Jo's kitchen table, hands wrapped around a hot drink, watching Jaxton cook dinner in the kitchen. There are a couple of steaks frying in one pan and fresh-cut potatoes frying in another, and it all smells incredible. My stomach is rumbling like crazy.

He's refused all my offers of help.

"I usually do all the cooking at home," I protested.

"And that's exactly why you're not going to lift a finger right now," he told me sternly. "You're going to sit right there and relax."

So, I'm following his orders. Except, I'm not relaxed at all. My whole body is tingling, throbbing with the after-effects of all the orgasms he gave me. Jaxton mated me. He was my first. He was my first and it was incredible. Even better than I imagined. His mouth between my legs, on my nipples. He knew exactly how to make my body sing. Then the big fierce thrust of his cock, pounding into me again and again. Muscles bunched, skin slick with fresh perspiration. All I could do was cling to him helplessly and come again, and again, and again. He was so wild and beastly, but so tender at the same time.

Afterwards, he held me in his arms for a long time, caressing me, telling me I'm beautiful, until our stomachs started to rumble.

Jaxton's broad back muscles ripple beneath his shirt as he moves around the tiny kitchenette like he's worked there a hundred times before. He thought of everything. He's brought a bunch of food, a new gas canister and cooking equipment, and he's made this little place so cozy. It really feels like our home. I wish, more than anything that we could just stay here together. Shut the world out and not worry about anything at all. But I can't…

I shake my head, dash the thought away. I'm determined not to give into the sadness that prickles at the edges of this beautiful moment. I've got tonight and tomorrow, and I'm going to pack a whole lifetime of happiness into these days.

Jaxton turns off the stove, slides the steaks onto two plates. "Ready," he says, flashing that sexy smile of his.

"Gosh, this looks fantastic," I groan as he puts a laden plate down in front of me.

He slides into the seat opposite and raises a glass of

red wine. It turns out Grandma Jo had a secret wine stash, and we've cracked open a bottle.

"Cheers. To us," he says.

"To us." I clink my glass against his and take a sip of the dark liquid.

I'm not used to drinking wine, but it feels real grownup sharing this experience with Jaxton. It's all so romantic. The low lighting; the fire burning in the corner; the candles on the table.

My mate's eyes burning into mine.

I love the way he's watching me, expectantly, as I take the first bite of steak. I know he took a lot of care with it.

I close my eyes blissfully. "It's... literally the best steak I've ever eaten."

"It's not." He's crooking an eyebrow dubiously.

"Yes, seriously. It's *so* good."

He allows himself a small smile. "I'm just happy if you like it."

I reach across the table and squeeze his hand. "Everything is perfect," I tell him. "I couldn't be happier."

Jaxton's smile gets bigger. "That's all that matter—"

He freezes. Then his smile drops and he jolts out of his seat.

"Huh? What's wrong?"

"I heard something." He dashes to the window, peers through the gap in the curtains. "Shouldn't have let my damn guard down," he mutters, peering out at the darkness.

I didn't hear anything. "You sure—?" I start to say.

Then I remember—he's a shifter. His hearing is probably a hundred times as sensitive as mine.

He goes to the door, and stands close, listening. Sniffing.

My heart hammers. Is it the cops again? Or my father? Did he somehow manage to make it here in the middle of a blizzard, furious that I disobeyed him? Doesn't seem possible…

With a roar, Jaxton tears open the door. "Caleb!" he bellows into the storm.

Caleb?

A moment later, something that looks like the abominable snowman hurtles to the door.

"What the hell are you doing here?" Jaxton hollers.

"Hey, bro." The snowman flashes a grin.

Jaxton's brother. My heartbeat slows.

"Wooh, it's wild out here!" He swipes snow off his face, and I make out longish, curly hair.

Jaxton looks extremely unimpressed. "Again, what are you doing here?" he growls through gritted teeth.

"I was planning to crash at yours, but I saw you weren't home, and I followed your truck over here. Sure hope I'm not disturbing anything." He peers around Jaxton's bulk, trying to get a better look at me.

"You are," Jaxton replies.

"Uh, sorry. Guess I'll go over to your place. Anything to eat in there?"

"Not really."

Caleb lifts his nose and scents the air. "That smells hella good. Can't do a lot of hunting in a blizzard."

"Just go sleep. I'll speak to you tomorrow," Jaxton snaps. I can almost feel the anger crackling off his body.

"Got any jerky? I haven't eaten for almost two days—"

"Don't give me that crap, Caleb. You've always been good at looking out for yourself."

"It's okay," I say quietly. "If you're worried about me —it's fine."

Jaxton slams the door in his brother's face. The moment his eyes meet mine, they turn soft, all frustration gone from them. "Rowan, this is your special evening. I want everything to be perfect. You don't know my brother. He pulls this kind of shit all the time."

"It is perfect," I tell him. "Just being here with you is enough. And I can only eat half my steak. He's welcome to the other half."

Jaxton looks from me, to my plate and back again, growling and muttering to himself. "You're too kind, you know that?" He darts forward and plants a kiss on my forehead. "Just one of the things I love about you."

Love—?

The word bounces around my head as he turns back to the door and heaves it open.

Did he really mean that? Things have happened so fast between Jaxton and me, but I love him, too. With all my heart. I feel like I've always loved him.

But should I tell him, before I have to walk out of his life forever?

Caleb doesn't wait to be invited in. He bursts through the door, shaking the snow off himself.

"Don't make a mess in here!" Jaxton bellows. "This isn't one of your flea-infested dives!"

"Sorry, sorry." Caleb tries to wipe the snow onto the mat more discreetly.

I giggle. There's something endearing about Jaxton's weary acceptance of his brother. Right away, I understand that Caleb is the younger brother, and Jaxton the responsible elder.

Caleb grabs a chair from the side of the room and drags it up to the table. Jaxton waits until he's more presentable before he introduces us.

"Rowan, this is my reprobate brother, Caleb. Caleb, this is..." He hesitates and my heart pounds. How is he planning to describe me?

"Your beautiful mate, of course," Caleb butts in.

While I'm still staring at him in amazement, he lifts my hand to his lips. "Very glad to make your acquaintance, Rowan."

Then he turns to Jaxton, with a flicker of hurt in his eyes. "Things happened fast, huh?"

Jaxton shakes his head and takes my other hand. "Nope. I found Rowan many years ago. I've just been waiting until I could be a worthy mate for her."

Caleb's eyes light up. "Sounds like a hell of a story."

I leap to my feet to grab a plate. My heart's beating so hard. *The way Jaxton's talking... I feel like I'm in a parallel universe where the clock's not ticking, and our future is stretching ahead of us...*

"Here you go." I put half my steak on Caleb's plate and add a big helping of potatoes.

He digs in right away, munching like a beast, while asking a ton of questions and waving his arms around.

"This man"—Caleb drops his silverware with a clatter and grabs Jaxton's arm—"is the best guy in the whole damn world. If you knew how we were raised..." he puffs his cheeks out. "I've been a beast all my life. A loser. But he's been in the military. He was their senior engineer. Decorated and shit. Now he makes a ton of money, without even having to leave his little mountain retreat—"

Jaxton tries to shush him up, but Caleb waves him off, shoves another piece of steak in his mouth. "And I've been a pain in his ass his whole life, let him down a bunch of times. But he's always got time for me. You won't find a better mate out there."

Jaxton clears his throat. "Enough of the sales pitch, Caleb." He looks so adorably embarrassed, my stomach tingles with love for him.

Caleb shrugs. "S'all true. Guess what I'm trying to say is *thank you*. Thank you for being an amazing brother. And thank you to you, Rowan, for so generously sacrificing your romantic evening for my uncivilized ass. You're an awesome person, and Jaxton is lucky to have you.

"Now, I'm going to leave you good people in peace."

Caleb shovels three more mouthfuls of steak and potatoes into his mouth, and gets to his feet.

"Key's under the wood pile, right?"

Jaxton nods.

"Catch you later." He charges to the cabin door,

and…he's gone. I stare at his retreating figure, feeling like a whirlwind just blew through.

Jaxton sighs. "I'm sorry about that."

I smile. "It's fine."

He shakes his head. "It's really not. But you were great with him. Thank you." He chafes my palm with his thumb. "Caleb can be *challenging*."

"He's had a rough time, too?" I say quietly.

"Yeah. He also went feral to avoid my father's rages, and he found it harder than I did to reclaim his human side. Then he lost his mate, and that really screwed him up."

"What happened?" I ask, thinking how young he is.

"Motorcycle accident. He got mixed up in an MC for a while. I don't know exactly what happened. She was on the back of his bike, and they had a crash. Seems like he wasn't at fault, but he blames himself anyway. Since then, he's been keeping himself busy raising hell. And I've been busy trying to keep him on the straight and narrow."

"Poor thing," I say. "But you've been doing a brilliant job,"

The ghost of a smile passes across his face. "You're a lovely person, you know that?"

I look at him questioningly.

"Plenty of people have run out of patience with him over the years."

I shrug. "Everyone deserves a second chance."

His smile gets wider. "I'm glad to hear you say that." His gaze passes over my empty plate. "Finished?"

"Sure have."

"Then come here." He holds his arms out and I get up and tumble into his lap.

For a long moment, he just holds me. I feel the rise and fall of his chest, hear his deep, growly breathing. Being in his arms, surrounded by him, is the best feeling in the world.

Then he cups my face in his big hands and draws me in. His mouth is hungry, passionate.

"Rowan, I want you so bad," he murmurs against my lips. He unfastens my button-down with impatient fingers, then he tugs my bra down, exposing my tits again. I sigh at his touch, at his callused fingers working my nipples into burning points of need. And his mouth... I love the way he sucks on them, one then the other, like he can't get enough of them.

When he slides a hand down the front of my panties, I cry out. I'm already wet for him. My pussy aching for his cock. He pushes one thick finger into me, and then another. I clench tight around them and start to ride him, wanting him to go deeper and deeper. I love the way his fingers curl into me, stimulating me in a different way from his cock.

My jeans and panties are sure getting in the way, though.

I stand up and strip them off, aware of his burning gaze watching my every move.

"So sexy," he growls.

I feel wild and a little dirty as I climb back on his lap, straddling him. When my bare pussy brushes the bulge in his pants, I let out a moan.

"That's it, baby. Ride it," he says, grasping my hips, making me ride his swollen cock, back and forth.

I'm so wet, aching so bad for him. I can't stand it anymore. I reach down and unzip his pants. His cock springs out, rock hard and even bigger than I remember. When I stroke it, it surges in my hand, and Jaxton's eyes burn, pure fire.

"Sit on it." He lifts me, maneuvering my hips until my pussy is perfectly lined up. Then he penetrates me. I slide down, onto his thick rod, feeling my muscles yielding to him as he goes deeper and deeper.

He's so big. It's hard to take all of him, But suddenly, all my weight lands on him and I gasp. So deep inside me. I swear he's buried up to my belly button.

"Fuck," he growls. Still inside me, he stands and plants my ass down on the table.

And he starts to fuck me like that. Holding my thighs wide, plowing into me, while I grip onto the edge of the tabletop for balance.

"You're mine, Rowan," he snarls into my ear. "This sweet pussy is mine."

"It's all yours," I tell him.

A sound of raw hunger breaks from his throat, and starts to screw me twice as hard. "I'm going to take this sweet little pussy every day. Fuck you till you can't take any more." His hands are rough on my tits, pinching, squeezing, and I love it. Love the fierceness in his face.

"I'll fill you with my seed again and again. And one day, when you're on heat, I'm gonna put my cubs inside you."

He's so deep inside me, spreading me wide open.

Possessing me. Owning me.

Every thrust sets me on fire. My pussy clenches tight around him.

He goes harder and harder, his cock so big, pounding, pounding into me.

"Jaxton!" I cry out. "I'm going to—"

"You're going to come around my cock?" he grunts. He cradles my head in his hands, looks right into my eyes. His dark eyes burn fierce. "That's right baby, I'm going to fuck this orgasm out of you." He leans back a little and watches his cock going in and out of my pussy.

That's so freaking hot. I let out a wild moan.

"Are you gonna come now?" he mutters. "Milk my cock with this tiny pussy of yours?"

I shudder all over. I love hearing these dirty words coming out of his mouth. A tremble starts up inside me. I let my head fall back, and give in to the blissful sensations. I can't think about anything else, apart from Jaxton's cock pushing inside me, filling me up. Making me his, over and over again.

"That's right, come for me," he growls, and finally, I come apart. Gasping and crying out, while this big man-beast holds me tight and hammers into me.

"So sexy, baby," he croons as my climax dies away. "So fucking hot." He rides me harder and harder. "My mate. All mine—" Suddenly, he lets out a roar, his hands biting into my hips. I feel his hot cum splashing inside me, flooding my womb.

I'm *his*, I think. I'll always be his, no matter what the rest of my life is like.

10

Rowan

 *N*othing is going to interrupt our last twenty-four hours together. Jaxton has threatened his brother with brutal consequences if he bothers us. And the blizzard will keep everybody else out. We're snowed in. No humans, no vehicles can make it to us. It's just Jaxton and I, together in Grandma Jo's cabin, cut off from the rest of the world.

Jaxton keeps the fire stoked up, and this little place is so warm and cozy. I keep pulling back the curtains and peeping outside, incredulous that it's so cold and wild out there, when in here is all warmth and love.

Love.

The word is constantly on my lips. But I can't tell Jaxton how I feel. Because in two days' time, I'm going to be given to another man and I'll never see him again.

Does he feel the same about me?

Every time he looks at me, his eyes glow with such intensity.

But I don't have the right to expect love from him, when I can't *really* be his.

All day long, he's the same as before. Kind, affectionate. Possessive. If he's sad this is our last day together, he doesn't show it.

Is he putting on a brave face, because he doesn't want to waste the last day?

Or maybe he's not so cut up about it after all. Maybe life will just go on for him.

And that's how it should be. I just want him to be happy. I know he needs to find his true mate and fall in love. And not some puny human, but a fierce shifter lady who deserves all his strength and protectiveness.

As much as the thought of him meeting another girl tears me apart.

We spend the whole time eating, talking, snuggling in bed, and mating, over and over again. We have sex so often, we don't need clothes. I just pad around naked, until he gets that look in his eye, and he possesses me again. On the bed, bent over the table. In the shower. On the rug in front of the fire.

He tells me he can't get enough of me, and I feel like a goddess under his gaze. Like someone special.

Such beautiful moments. And I'm trying my best to live in the moment, but I can't forget that the clock is ticking. Every minute counting off our time together.

Every kiss, every touch, every thrust is bittersweet. A little piece of ecstasy, and a dagger in my heart.

I wish so bad that this was forever.

If only Charlie was safe, I wouldn't go back. I'd leave my father to deal with the consequences of his greed and cruelty by himself.

But she's not safe. As long as DiMarco doesn't have me, she'll always be in danger.

And I'm the only one who can fix that.

* * *

In the evening, I insist on cooking—some meat, tomato sauce and pasta dish. Not as tasty as Jaxton's steaks, but he devours it, making sexy sounds of appreciation.

"You'll have to teach me that recipe," he says.

We've been saying things like this to each other the whole time. Discussing a future that we both know can never happen. At the beginning it was kind of fun, but now it's killing me.

That night, he takes his time with me, undressing me tenderly, then licking my pussy until I come three times. And then he fucks me long and hard, in ten different positions, before finishing from behind with his teeth grazing the back of my neck. He's done this a bunch of times now, and I know what it means—he wants to mark me with his teeth. But he always holds back, then makes a sound like it's costing him a lot. Like the man and animal are at war. I want to have his mark. I Imagine having it there all my life, comforting me. But I wonder what it would mean to him—if it would mean he couldn't take another.

When we're both thoroughly sated, and my body can't take any more pleasure, Jaxton wraps me up in his arms, and pulls the thick comforter around us, and we fall asleep.

But half an hour later, I'm awake again. Thinking about tomorrow. Thinking that when I wake up, it's the last time I'll ever see him.

I MUST'VE DRIFTED off at some point, because when I next open my eyes, it's morning. I stare out at the little crack of daylight between the curtains, and a feeling starts to grow inside me.

How could I even think of leaving Jaxton? He's my mate. The moment I laid eyes on him, I knew he was the one. I felt it when I saw him standing there, half-naked in the snow, holding the axe. He's mine. And I'm his. And I'll do whatever it takes to be with him. Fight anyone. Even my father. But first—I'm gonna wake him up with a kiss. I turn over onto my left side, already reaching for him.

But he's not there, and the sheets on his side of the bed are cold.

Weird. Did he go to the bathroom?

No, the bathroom door's wide open. A bad feeling is building inside me. I jerk upright, dart across the room and check it anyway. Then I rush back to bed, confused, stupidly believing that he might still be there after all.

Maybe he went out early? Went off to do some beary thing like hunting in the woods or something. But...

there's a piece of paper on the kitchen table. Heart hammering, I unfold it with trembling fingers, already suspecting what it's going to say:

Good morning, Sweet Rowan,

The snowplows had been out already, and the road is clear all the way down, but please drive safe.

Jaxton xxx

THAT'S ALL. Stomach lurching, I read it over and over, trying to understand his words. But my brain won't untangle them. He's not coming back. He left already. There's no secret meaning in there. It's pretty darn obvious. This is goodbye.

My throat closes up and the back of my eyes sting. I swallow hard, take a couple of deep breaths. He decided to leave early to spare us the pain of parting. I guess it makes sense. It's the kind of thing I might have done, too.

Well, I've just got to go and tell him my plan. I hunt around for the clothes I haven't worn for a couple of days, and yank them on. Then, I grab my coat and car keys and hurtle out of the cabin.

Whoa, he's right. The snowplows have been out. In place of gigantic snowdrifts is a well-plowed road. I run to my car, jump in and speed over to Jaxton's cabin.

I'm halfway there when I see that his truck is not parked in the driveway.

My heart plummets.

He's gone. He's really gone.

I pull up in front of his place and pick my way

through the deep snow covering his pathway. I'm trying not to notice that there are no fresh footprints in the snow, and his cabin looks dark inside. I pound on his door desperately, but only silence greets me.

Fuck.

I collapse against the door, sliding down until my ass hits the step.

How could I have been so dumb? I had this amazing, amazing guy, and I was so caught up with my father's ultimatum that I didn't think there could be another way, until it was too late. What an idiot I am letting my father push me and Charlie around like this! He doesn't own me, or her.

But now I've lost Jaxton, too. I replay last night in my mind. Was he waiting for me to say something? To say I wasn't going to go after all? I think of all those moments when we stared silently into each other's eyes. I was full of sadness and regret, and I assumed he was, too.

But was he thinking, surely she's got to change her mind now? Surely if she cared about me enough, she'd find a way? I ached to hear *I love you* from him. But he wouldn't say the words. Maybe because he thought I didn't deserve to hear them. And he was right.

I stare out at the blanket of snow stretching in all directions. My instinct is to go look for him, but where? He could be anywhere in this wilderness.

I haul myself to my feet. I need to get back home, before Dad does something to Charlie. He warned me not to test him and I know what he's like. Even refusing to come back early was a lot more than anything I've done before. I've got to keep her safe.

I trudge back to the car.

Back at Grandma Jo's cabin, I pack my things fast. The fire has burned out now, and the room is cold again. I take one last long look around this dear little place, tears blurring my vision.

"Thank you, Grandma Jo," I whisper. "For these four beautiful days with Jaxton. I will always treasure them."

I leave the door unlocked, in case Jaxton wants to use this place. It will make me happy knowing that he's here. Then I throw all my stuff in the car, and I start the long snowy drive back home.

The GPS says four hours, thirty minutes. Will it be enough time to decide whether to go on the run with Charlie and subject her to a difficult life, or go ahead with my marriage to DiMarco?

Well, it better be. Because it's all the time I have.

THE SUN HAS CLIMBED to its highest point in the wintry sky as I pull into my hometown again. My stomach is in a knot, and I'm sick with nerves.

All I know is that there's no way I can give myself to DiMarco. You don't find your mate, and then go do something like that. Before I met Jaxton, the thought of being with DiMarco was repulsive and awful. But now Jaxton has made me his, it's impossible.

I'm gonna go in there, take Charlie, and run like hell. Whatever it takes. Then, one day in the future, if I ever feel like we're out of danger, I'll go find Jaxton as a free woman. And if he's already found himself a lady bear, then fair enough. I'll never find another mate, because Jaxton has my heart forever. But at least I will have protected the memory of us.

I turn onto the street where our family home is, but I park up a couple of hundred yards away. I'm hoping against hope that my father will be out at a meeting and I can just snatch Charlie.

But when I approach the driveway, the sight of three unfamiliar black cars parked there stops me in my tracks. My throat tightens. DiMarco and his associates? Every nerve in my body tells me to run away. To get back into my car and drive the hell away from here. But Charlie must be in there.

Heart hammering, I dash to the front door. It's a little open. I push it wider and slip through. At the end of the hallway is the dining room. The door is also open. I catch sight of three men in expensive-looking black suits. They are standing around my father, who's seated at the table, holding his head in his hands. I creep closer, staying out of sight.

"Guess I don't have a choice, do I?" I hear him saying. There are some papers in front of him. Looks like a contract or something. My mind whirrs. What's going on? If this was DiMarco's contract of sale, surely my father would be in high spirits. But I've never seen him sound so... beaten.

"Well, you could still sell your daughter, instead," a voice says.

A very familiar voice.

What? It's not coming from the three men in black. It's coming from the other side of the room. Dizzy with confusion, I burst through the door.

There's Jaxton, standing in the middle of the dining room, thumbs tucked into the waistband of his jeans. So much bigger than the rest of them, and perfectly at ease in our McMansion.

His eyes turn on to me, and the love and regard in them almost makes my heart stop beating.

Then he winks at me. I get it.

He holds out a hand. Instinctively, I run over and squeeze it with my own.

My father raises his head. There's a flicker of hope in his eyes. "I could still do that instead?" he asks.

Jaxton lets out a roar. "No, you piece of shit. Of course, you can't sell your own daughter! I was being facetious."

The three men turn to me. "Rowan Anderson?" One of them asks.

"Yes, that's me," I say. "Where's Charlie?"

"She's in her room," Jaxton replies.

"What the hell's going on here?"

"It turns out that your father's creditor, DiMarco, is a very dangerous man," Jaxton says. "In an interesting turn of events, the FBI has been wanting to get their hands on him for a long time. And if your father is willing to testify against him, he can go into witness protection. His debts will be cancelled, and he'll be free."

"Free? Like hell I will!" my father snarls.

"Your choice, buddy," one of the FBI agents says.

"You can either be free in the little town of West Butt-fuck, Oklahoma, or you can be dead."

My father grumbles and scrubs at his face.

Jaxton takes my other hand and turns me, so I'm looking at him directly. "The bad news is that you and Charlie are going to have to disappear for a while, too."

My mouth falls open. "Not with Dad. No way!"

Jaxton shakes his head slowly. "Of course not. Considering your father's, uh, *parenting skills*, the FBI has offered to find you a separate safehouse. But,"—a smile tugs at the corners of his lips—"I volunteered to take care of you both. Take you someplace where DiMarco's henchmen aren't going to find you."

I cast a glance at the three agents for confirmation. The closest one nods his assent. Jaxton is in charge, I realize. These three federal agents are letting him do all the talking. I'm starting to understand that there's more to his military past than he made out.

I turn back to Jaxton. "You're saying we can be together?"

"Yes, honey. That's exactly what I'm saying."

My heart leaps. "Oh, my god—" I whisper.

"You might have to change your names, et cetera," he cuts in with a frown. "Your life will be real different from how it was before—"

"Sounds great to me," says an upbeat, sassy voice. I turn and watch as Charlie enters the room. Her eyes are bright, and she looks lighter than I've seen in a long, long time. Well, ever since she realized what a prime asshole my father is, really. She's carrying a large holdall.

"Ready when you are," she says.

"We need to get going right now," Jaxton cuts in. "Your father has confirmed that DiMarco knows nothing about the cabin and we need to make sure it stays that way. I'm sorry about this. I wish you had more time to pack your stuff."

"Not a problem," I say. "Let me just grab one thing."

I dash upstairs, lift up a rug, two loose floorboards, and take out a wooden box—the home of all my most precious keepsakes. Cards, notes, photos, things my mom made for me over the years. I shove it under my arm and sprint back down the stairs.

Then I pause and take one last look at my father. He's been in my life for twenty years, and it's weird how little I feel for this broken man, sobbing over the table.

"Goodbye, father," I say to him. "Not that you deserve to be called a father. You've dishonored the promise you made to our mom to take care of us. And you'll carry that shame with you for the rest of your life. But now I'm going to forget that I ever had a father."

"We'll be in touch," one of the agents tells us, and Jaxton sweeps us out of the house. His big truck is waiting in the garage, and he makes us duck down low in the back seats until we are out of the city limits.

And we're off—retracing our path back to Grandma Jo's dear little cabin. The sky is blue and the sun is glistening off the endless fields of white. Charlie chatters excitedly for the first fifteen minutes, then her head starts to nod and she falls asleep.

"What did you do?" I ask Jaxton in a low voice.

He takes his eyes off the road long enough to flash

me his sexy smile. "What makes you think I did anything?"

"Well, apart from the fact that you're here, right now, it seems like a hell of a coincidence that the FBI just happened to appear today."

He sighs. "You're too smart for your own good, you know that?"

"Yup." I shrug happily, knowing he means it in the best possible way.

"So, I did some research on DiMarco. I assessed his vulnerabilities, and it turned out there were a ton of them. Then I made a couple of calls to some old connections of mine. That's all."

I draw in a deep breath and let it out again. For the first time in forever, it doesn't catch in my chest. "You're amazing," I say. "And thank you."

"Any time." He takes my hand and squeezes it. "Any time at all."

When our eyes meet, my heart explodes with love for him. I open my mouth to say the words at last—

"I'm sorry I left before you woke up," he says at the same time.

"Oh, it's fine," I manage to say.

His head snaps toward mine. "It's not fine, is it?"

Damn, there he is, picking up on my thoughts again.

"I thought I'd never see you again," I admit.

"What?"

"Yeah. That note you left me. It seemed so final—"

"Damnit." He shakes his head. "What a freaking idiot I was. Guess I was so focused on meeting up with the agents, I wasn't thinking straight. I'm so sorry, Rowan. I promise you'll never have another moment of doubt about me again."

He flicks on the blinker and pulls over on the side of the road. "C'mere." He unfastens our seatbelts and draws me into his arms.

"Rowan Anderson," he whispers, holding me tight. "You're my mate, and I love you so much. All I want is to spend my life protecting you and making you happy."

My eyes prickle. "I love *you* so much," I whisper, and our lips meet in a passionate kiss.

My stomach is full of butterflies and I'm already so *happy*. I can't wait for us all to start our new lives together.

EPILOGUE

Three months later

*I*t's buzzing in Poppy's Little Coffee House, just the way I like it. The tables are full of locals chatting and sipping the drinks I just made, and there are several people waiting in line at the counter.

But in between whipping up cappuccinos and peppermint lattes, my eyes keep drifting to the clock. It's almost three p.m., and he's close by.

The mark on the back of my neck is tingling, as it always does when he's near.

A shadow falls across the counter, and I look up.

His familiar bulk fills the doorway, while his dark gaze sweeps the room, zoning in on me.

My mate. My love. My heart flutters.

I love the way that every female eye turns in his direction, but he only has eyes for me.

"Hey, baby." Jaxton strides over to me. Then he cups my face in his big hands and plants a kiss on my lips. "God, I missed you," he growls.

"Awww," one of the customers says. I love how demonstrative he is. How he makes it clear to everyone that I'm his.

"I missed you, too," I say, my heart skittering. Three months together and everything still feels brand new.

"Hey, sis." Charlie emerges from behind him. She slips behind the counter and ties on her apron. Her name badge says Jennifer, but she doesn't care. She picked it because it was the name of her imaginary friend when she was small. She's the same perky, funny teen she's always been. Except now, she's no longer carrying the burden that my father dumped on both of us all our lives. I can't believe how fast she's settled in here. I was worried she'd hate living on the outskirts of a small town, but she thinks it's the cutest thing ever, and she's already made a bunch of friends.

"You about done?" Jaxton says.

I grin. "Why so impatient?"

He gives a little growl. "You know why."

A shiver goes through me.

Every day, he's so eager to get me home, he just about hauls me out of the shop.

I hand over to Charlie, then I tear off my apron and hang it up out the back.

She waves goodbye, and gets to work on the espresso machine.

Doing shifts at Poppy's is working out perfectly for us. I do forty hours a week, while Charlie does twenty, fitting her shifts around her schoolwork. I told her she doesn't need to work at all, but she insisted. She likes having her independence, and I think she really enjoys her job, too.

Jaxton drives extra fast along the little road that leads to Wilder's Edge, throwing his truck through the bends. It's a perfect spring day, the sky is bright blue and the trees are starting to get their leaves. When Grandma Jo's cabin comes into view, my heart lifts. It's our cabin now—mine and Jaxton's. Charlie mostly stays in the cabin Jaxton built to be near me. I often smile to think how remote it seemed that time I collapsed in the snow while trying to make it to his place. It's only a couple of hundred yards away. Far enough to give Charlie her own space, but near enough for us to hang out at each other's places all the time. We feel safe here. The FBI has been keeping us updated. They've already rounded up DiMarco and his key associates. Offering immunity brought plenty of snitches out of the woodwork. They're confident that no one is looking for us. And if anyone were to come looking—well, we've got a big, growly bear to protect us.

Jaxton pulls up in front of the cabin and I bound to the door, already fizzing with anticipation. I'm as hungry for him as he is for me.

Indoors, I strip off my shirt and reach for the button on my jeans. Then I hesitate—

I tilt my head to one side, studying him. He's standing in the middle of the cabin, watching me. Hands on his hips, that telltale bulge in his pants, which says he's dying to be inside me. But there's something else in his eyes—a different kind of excitement.

"What is it?" I demand.

"What's what?"

I narrow my eyes. "Don't act innocent with me. I know you're hiding something."

He groans. "Sometimes I wish you didn't know me so well." He goes to the big old leather bag that he carries his laptop in, and pulls out a glossy magazine. I frown. Some kind of brochure?

Brookville Community College, it reads.

"Remember when you told me you didn't have dreams?" he says.

I raise an eyebrow. "Maybe."

"I knew you were lying."

"You did? How gentlemanly of you not to mention it."

He grins. "The college is two towns over. It's supposed to be a good one. Thought you might find some classes you're interested in. So you can finish up your degree."

He looks so bashful, I rush over and hug him. "Thank you," I say. I skim the contents page. Majors like conservation and environmental science catch my eye. I have been thinking about finishing my degree, but I've lost interest in my old major of marketing and communications. Now I'm living in this beautiful wilderness, working in nature is the only thing that makes sense.

"Maybe you'll take a look at it later." I hear the impatience in his voice as he reaches for the brochure. But I turn away from him, holding it out of reach. "After what?" I ask innocently.

A growl escapes his lips. "After I've made you come all over my cock, of course."

I purse my lips and start leafing through the magazine, ignoring the fact that my whole body is throbbing with need for him. "Looks real interesting, though."

His growl turns into a roar. In a single movement, he snatches me up in his arms and dumps me onto the bed.

I scream in delight. And then I go still as he strips his shirt and his jeans off. He's not wearing underwear, as usual. He's all naked and ready for me.

The world can wait. Nothing matters as much as being with my gorgeous, growly mate.

THE END

READ THE OTHER BOOKS IN THE SERIES

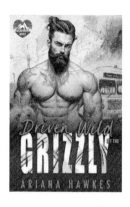

If you like fated-mate romances, with plenty of V-card fun and tons of feels, check out the other books in the series at:

arianahawkes.com/obsessed-mountain-mates

READ MY OTHER OBSESSED MATES SERIES

If you like steamy insta-love romance, featuring obsessed, growly heroes who'll do anything for their mates, check out my Obsessed Mates series. All books are standalone and can be read in any order.

Get started at arianahawkes.com/obsessed-mates

READ THE REST OF MY CATALOGUE

MateMatch Outcasts: a matchmaking agency for beasts, and the women tough enough to love them.

★★★★★ "A super **exciting, funny, thrilling, suspenseful and steamy shifter romance series**. The characters jump right off the page!"

★★★★★ "**Absolutely Freaking Fantastic**. I loved every single word of this story. It is so full of **exciting twists that will keep you guessing until the very end** of this book. I can't wait to see what might happen next in this series."

Ragtown is a small former ghost town in the mountains, populated by outcast shifters. It's a secretive place, closed-off to the outside world - until someone sets up a secret mail-order bride service that introduces women looking for their mates.

Get started at arianahawkes.com/matematch-outcasts

MY OTHER MATCHMAKING SERIES

My bestselling *Shiftr: Swipe Left For Love* series features Shiftr, the secret dating app that brings curvy girls and sexy shifters their perfect match! Fifteen books of totally bingeworthy reading — and my readers tell me that Shiftr is their favorite app ever! ;-) Get started at arianahawkes. com/shiftr

★★★★★ "**Shiftr is one of my all-time favorite series**! The stories are funny, sweet, exciting, and scorching hot! And they will **keep you glued to the pages**!"

★★★★★ "**I wish I had access to this app**! Come on, someone download it for me!"

Get started at arianahawkes.com/shiftr

CONNECT WITH ME

If you'd like to be notified about new releases, giveaways and special promotions, you can sign up to my mailing list at arianahawkes.com/mailinglist. You can also follow me on BookBub and Amazon at:

bookbub.com/authors/ariana-hawkes

amazon.com/author/arianahawkes

Thanks again for reading – and for all your support!

Yours,

Ariana

* * *

USA Today bestselling author Ariana Hawkes writes spicy romantic stories with lovable characters, plenty of suspense, and a whole lot of laughs. She told her first story at the age of four, and has been writing ever since, for both work and pleasure. She lives in Massachusetts with her husband and two huskies.

www.arianahawkes.com

GET TWO FREE BOOKS

Join my mailing list and get two free books.

 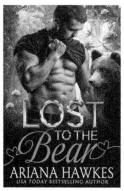

Once Bitten Twice Smitten

A 4.5-star rated, comedy romance featuring one kickass roller derby chick, two scorching-hot Alphas, and the naughty nip that changed their lives forever.

Lost To The Bear

He can't remember who he is. Until he meets the woman he'll never forget.

Get your free books at arianahawkes.com/freebook

READING GUIDE TO ALL OF MY BOOKS

Obsessed Mates

Her River God Wolf

Her Biker Wolf

Her Alpha Neighbor Wolf

Her Bad Boy Trucker Wolf

Her Second Chance Wolf

Her Convict Wolf

Obsessed Mountain Mates

Driven Wild By The Grizzly

Snowed In With The Grizzly

Chosen By The Grizzly

Shifter Dating App Romances

Shiftr: Swipe Left for Love 1: Lauren

Shiftr: Swipe Left for Love 2: Dina

Shiftr: Swipe Left for Love 3: Kristin

Shiftr: Swipe Left for Love 4: Melissa

Shiftr: Swipe Left for Love 5: Andrea

Shiftr: Swipe Left for Love 6: Lori

Shiftr: Swipe Left for Love 7: Adaira

Shiftr: Swipe Left for Love 8: Timo

Shiftr: Swipe Left for Love 9: Jessica

Shifter Holiday Romances

Bear My Holiday Hero

Ultimate Bear Christmas Magic Boxed Set Vol. 1

Ultimate Bear Christmas Magic Boxed Set Vol. 2